TOUCH OF MAGIC

STELLA RAINBOW

CONTENTS

DEDICATION

Dedicated to:
My younger brother, who is to me what Joy is to Jai. I love you,
little one.
My Dad, who is my real hero.

GLOSSARY

Old Language of the Mages

Semlee: A familiar; an animal companion.

Semnyar: A mate; A person's other half chosen by fate.

Hindi Words:

Ma: Mom.

Beta: Child/Kid.

*Bhai:*Brother.

Chhote: Little one.

Paneer: Cottage Cheese.

Ek: One.

**Jai says 'Gods' because the Hindu mythology consists of many Gods and Deities.*

ONE

Jai

I gasped as I took another step, my lungs burning with the need for oxygen. You can do it, I told myself. Three more blocks and I'd be home. This was as far as I'd gotten every other time without having to take a break, but I was determined to make it home today. I did not want this illness to take over more of my life than it already had. Walking Padfoot—I most definitely named him after Sirius Black from Harry Potter—was one of the few opportunities I had to get out these days. I would not let my fucked up heart and lungs take that away from me too.

The weather was nice today, the sky cloudy with the promise of rain and the air a cool breeze. The pleasant weather was what had led to me doing this in the middle of the day. Usually, I waited until the sun had set before going out, but I couldn't resist the allure of the cloudy skies and the cool breeze. It was one mile. A one-mile walk that my shitty body couldn't manage without making me look like I'd been running for hours. I'd been out for ten minutes at the most and yet, I was already exhausted. I tightened my grip on Padfoot's leash almost reflexively. He wouldn't run away, I knew that. He didn't care that I walked at a snail's pace. He was just happy to be out and about.

I bit my lip as a wave of dizziness washed over me and the next thing I knew, I was on my knees on the sidewalk. My lungs were burning as if they'd been deprived of oxygen for years, my heart thudding at an uneven pace in my ears. It had been one fucking mile and I couldn't even do that. Fuck. Padfoot shuffled closer to me, licking the side of my face and whimpering against me. I wanted to comfort him and tell him I was okay, but I couldn't make my body work.

I closed my eyes as I tried to keep my emotions in check. Getting frustrated would only hurt me more. My legs felt too weak to get up. God, maybe mom was right. Maybe I wasn't made to do this adulting shit.

No, I shook off the thought. I would do this. I was tired of being tired. I was tired of being the sick kid, the one who could do nothing. I took a deep breath and forced myself to stand up, slumping against the fence of the house I'd stopped in front of. It looked exactly like my house—like all the houses in this row of cul-de-sacs—but unlike my place, this house was surrounded in greenery. There were so many bushes and plants outside it that it was basically shrouded in greenery. I didn't even notice the man walking toward me until he was standing right before me with a concerned look on his face.

I craned my neck to look up at him, since I was still leaning heavily against the fence. I swallowed hard when my eyes fell on him. Wow. The guy was hot with a capital H. It figured that our first meeting had to be with me almost dying on his sidewalk. I never had a chance, anyway. Not that I knew if he was even into guys. He was gorgeous, though, with soft blond hair that fell to his shoulders and eyes that were a strange mix of brown and green. He extended a hand as if to touch me before pulling away. "Are you okay?"

What was up with me? My thoughts were heading to places I hadn't thought about in a long time. One look at this gorgeous guy and I was thinking about things I'd given up on ever experiencing. Ugh, I needed to get myself under control. The last thing I needed was to go mooning over some guy I'd just met.

I nodded, still a bit breathless. I wasn't sure if the breathlessness had to do with the walk or this man, but I forced myself to take a deep breath. I smiled at him. "Yeah, I'm okay. Sorry about that."

I went to straighten up and my body betrayed me yet again, making me stumble. I would've fallen flat on my face except a sturdy pair of arms grabbed me, steadying me. My heart started racing again, except this time it was for a completely different reason. I breathed in the scent of grass and honey and, for some reason, it helped calm my nerves. His hand was warm against me and my skin tingled where he'd touched me. The sensation was there even after he pulled away and I rubbed my arm to get rid of the goosebumps that had popped up.

Once I was upright, I realized the dizziness had all but disappeared and I felt much better than I had when I'd stopped. Seemed like my body had had enough time to catch up and hoard some oxygen. Who knew all it would need was me talking to a hot as sin guy to bring my body back on track? Yeah, right.

"Uh, thanks."

"No problem! My name's Raphael. I live right here." He hooked a thumb backwards to point at the greenland he'd stepped out of. My mind was still stuck on his name.

"The angel of healing," I found myself saying, and then I blushed. Fuck. Shut the hell up, Jai. He didn't need to know about my absolute nerdiness or about my obsession with mythology and fantasy. Godsdamnit.

"The one and the same," Raphael said a wink, a cheery smile lighting up his face. Wow, he was even prettier when he smiled. Shit, I needed to get out of here before I blurted something else out.

"Um, I'm gonna go. Thanks for your help."

"No worries! Hey, I'm new in town and since we're neighbors, would you like to hang out sometime?"

I nodded, even as I scoffed mentally. No one really wanted to get to know me. Or if they did, they lost interest as soon as they realized how much baggage I carried. Just how long could you be friends with someone who constantly canceled or backed out of plans? How long could you hang onto a friend who never wanted to do anything or was a homebody? Their words, not mine. I wished I could be a good friend to people, but I just couldn't. My fucked-up health wouldn't let me. The too many bad days I had to deal with wouldn't let me.

Making friends was not for me. Unless it was friends online who could only talk to me and never had to deal with all my daily issues. It was just as well. I didn't need friends who weren't at least willing to understand what it was like to be me.

"Sure, yeah. Maybe later." I waved at him and started walking, keeping my pace steady so as not to enrage my lungs again. Padfoot kept up a steady pace beside me, like I knew he would. Once I made it home, I'd treat myself to a tall glass of ice tea and a marathon of movies or shows. What would it be today? Avengers? Brooklyn 99?

"Hey, wait!" Raphael called out, and I looked over my shoulder at him with a raised brow. He stood there with his hands in his pockets, slouched over one side, and a crooked smile on his face. He looked like he was posing for some fashion magazine... except for the ratty t-shirt and jeans he wore. Was that mud on his clothes?

"You never told me your name."

I smiled at him, remembering that I'd been too caught up in the meaning of his name to give him the same courtesy. "It's Jai."

Raphael smiled widely at me as he spoke, pronouncing my name perfectly. "It was nice to meet you, Jai. I hope I'll see you again soon."

I shot him a smile before looking away so he wouldn't see my flustered state. He wasn't flirting, was he? Nah, my subconscious told me. No one in their right mind would flirt with me. The thought had nothing to do with self-esteem issues—or maybe it did. Fuck, I didn't even know anymore—and everything to do with the fact that I looked like a kid despite being twenty-three. Oh, and everything about me screamed baggage. There was no way he was the least bit interested in me. No fucking way.

Why was I still thinking about him?

Raphael

I watched him walk away, my palms still tingling from when I'd touched him. Even though the touch had lasted for only a few seconds, it had told me a lot more than I'd expected it to. I'd almost jerked my hand away in surprise when my magic had reacted to him. The reaction had been unlike anything I'd ever experienced. My magic had rushed towards him with a speed that had shocked me. Though I'd pulled away as quickly as I could, I'd still sensed something. He was sick and whatever his illness was, it was killing him, bit by bit. I didn't know why my magic had reacted the way it had, but I didn't think it meant anything. It was probably acting up like it did sometimes. If I had more power like the rest of my family did, I would have been able to tell what he was suffering from. I could've even tried to heal him.

But I wasn't like my mom, or dad, or even my little sister. I was Raph, the runt of the litter, the one who had no powers except for the inherent magic all mages carried. I was weak and useless and all the words the people in Ravenshire had whispered behind me—or to my face if they were my parents.

I shook off the dark thoughts because, rationally, I knew it wasn't my fault. Magic wasn't something you could increase with practice. You could get better at using it, yes, but the power came from your blood, from your genes. I knew it wasn't my fault that my blood lacked the power the rest of my family had in abundance. Sometimes it was hard to accept. It was even harder to accept that my own family saw nothing in me but a failure. They were probably happy that their disgrace of a son had left the island.

My thoughts turned back to the man I'd just met as I walked back into the house. When I'd first seen him the day I moved here, I'd thought he was a kid, a teenager at the most. But something about him had stuck with me and I'd soon realized he was actually quite older than he looked. I'd found myself climbing up the tree in my backyard every evening to watch him walk his huge husky dog more times than I could count. I'd wanted to approach him but hadn't known how. Even today, I wouldn't have met him if he hadn't broken his routine and come out earlier than usual. I'd been planting some more shrubs in the small garden when I'd heard movement and spotted him on his knees on the sidewalk. It had taken me a few minutes to approach him because I'd been shocked, worried, and also a little confused.

I'd gotten my first real look at him when I'd approached him and what I saw almost stole my breath. He'd been dressed in a baggy hoodie and jeans that looked a size too big on him and he was so thin he almost looked malnourished. The look in his deep brown eyes, though...that was the weariness only someone who'd been dealing with pain or suffering for a long time would have in their eyes. I'd know, I saw that look every time I came across a mirror.

Something about him had resonated with me. I felt like if we got a chance to talk, we'd discover we were similar in a lot of ways. But then again, he'd blown me off when I'd asked him if he wanted to hang out. I'd felt like it was something he did a lot, but what if he really wasn't interested in hanging out with me?

Even so, I knew that I couldn't leave him alone. I'd seen something else in his eyes in that split second before he'd turned away. Something I related to only too well: loneliness. I felt like he could do with having a friend, or at least someone to talk to. Honestly, so could I.

Neya, the squirrel who had taken residence under my roof, scampered up my arm and settled herself on my shoulder. Her bushy tail tickled my ear as I reached up to pet her.

"Hello, Miss Neya. What did you do today?" I'd found the squirrel in my backyard the day I moved in. Somehow, she'd broken her leg and ended up sprawled at the base of the large oak tree in my backyard. I'd taken her in and patched her up, though it had taken me some time to realize that my magic worked on her. The day she'd started hopping around and moving without pain, I'd felt such a rush of pride and joy at having helped her. At that moment, I'd realized how my parents must feel when they healed someone, and I'd wished for the millionth time that I could do the same. I could heal animals, though, and that was better than nothing. Right?

Neya chattered at me, her little paw gripping my ear and making me laugh. I wasn't sure if it was because I'd healed her or because she was just friendly, but Neya had decided to adopt me once she'd healed. Who was I to stop her from loving on me? At least someone valued my power now, flimsy as it may be.

I pulled her into my palm, grinning when she immediately grabbed my thumb. Leaning forward, I pressed a kiss on top of her head, chuckling when she swatted at me with her tail. "Alright, scamp. Don't go into the laundry room again or it won't be my fault if you end up in the washing machine!"

I placed her on the floor, and she immediately scampered towards the kitchen area. I had a dish of nuts for her in there and I knew she would help herself to it before escaping to her tree. I shook my head as I got to my feet and looked around the place that was now my home. It was bare at the moment, just a couch and a coffee table I'd bought a few days ago. I didn't like the lack of greenery.

The first thing I'd done when I moved in last week was buy a lot of bushes and plants for my yard. Looking around at my bare living room, I felt like I needed some indoor plants, too. Ravenshire had been full of greenery and though I definitely didn't miss the people, I yearned to be back in Ravenshire. It was a small island, but it was the most beautiful place I'd ever seen. Ravenshire was the only reason I'd stuck around my parents for a whole century and a half. If I hadn't loved the island so much, I'd have moved to Mistvale a lot sooner.

I blew out a breath as I walked into the kitchen, wondering what I was supposed to do now. For the last one hundred and fifty years—yes, I'm that old, but I look like I'm in my mid-twenties. Cool trick, huh?—I'd lived in my parents' house and assisted them in whatever way I could, which wasn't usually much. They were rich, so I'd always had enough money. Most of that money was now invested in different avenues, leaving me with a nice safety net to fall back on.

I'd left my parents with a brief letter telling them I'd had it with them treating me like I didn't matter. I'd asked them to not try to contact me, but I'd hoped they would. I'd hoped, in some small part of me, that they would care enough to at least call me. One week later, I was still waiting for that call.

I didn't regret my decision, though. Being here all alone was still better than the verbal torture. I missed Ravenshire, but maybe I'd be able to make a home here in Mistvale.

TWO

Raphael

I grinned as I looked around the living room. It had taken me almost a week to get this place just right. The house I'd bought on the edge of the Silent Creek Park was small, but it was home. Now, a week and a half after moving here, I finally felt like this place was mine. I'd spent the past week making sure every aspect of this place reflected me, and I couldn't stop smiling as I looked around the place.

The sliding glass door that led into the backyard was open so Neya could come and go as she wished, and I'd hung some cute, cream-colored lace curtains to pretty the place a bit. The couch I'd gotten was also cream colored, and green throw pillows covered half of it, giving it a comfy feel. The wall behind the couch had a nice set of hexagonal frames that I'd picked up at the market, and I'd placed small potted plants inside each frame with green vines and climbers hanging out of them, giving the room the greenery I needed. My magic was attuned to nature, and keeping myself surrounded by greenery helped keep my energy full. It wasn't like I had much use of what powers I had, but living among plants was comforting and I'd always felt more at home surrounded by them.

I'd placed some taller show plants in the corners of the rooms, with a few herb plants in pots I'd hung from the ceiling. I wasn't sure what a human would think if they ever saw my place. Did common humans have so many plants in their house? Would they think I was crazy or just a nature freak?

I shook my head as my thoughts drifted back to the human who had fallen on his knees in front of my house a week ago. I had still watched him every evening since that day, though I honestly hadn't meant to turn into a stalker. I was just a bit worried about him because he was clearly sick. Coming from a family of healers, I wasn't in the habit of ignoring someone who needed help. At least, that was the reason I gave myself when I found my thoughts returning to him again and again. Something about him had stuck with me. Part of me yearned to go check up on him, just to make sure he was okay. I didn't know why, but I needed to know he was okay. I felt restless at the idea that he might be in pain. It was like an itch under my skin that I just couldn't get rid of and it seemed to grow worse the longer I went without seeing him.

Groaning in frustration, I walked into the backyard, smiling as a calm washed over me once I reached the oak tree. The tree was old and huge, and it had been the reason I bought this exact house. The old owners had been planning to chop the poor thing down because apparently, people wouldn't buy the house with the tree behind it. I'd taken one look at the gorgeous monstrosity and I'd known I needed to save it. I'd made an offer without even going inside the house, my only focus being the tree stayed the way it was.

The tree reminded me a little of the enormous willow tree we had in Ravenshire, right by the shrine of Elder Rainer. Elder

Rainer had been the mage who'd discovered Ravenshire some five hundred years ago and turned it into a safe—ha!—haven for all the mages. His semlee—the animal companion every mage, who was *worthy of them,* was gifted with—had been a raven, which was how the name Ravenshire came to be, if the stories were to be believed. The shrine of Elder Rainer stood right in the center of the island. The town wrapped all around it with circular, winding streets.

The willow tree had been the perfect look out. We'd climb up its branches, hanging on with our toes. From the top, we could almost always see the entire island. The stone mansion belonging to the Romanov family, the docks and huts near the lakes that were the home of the few water mages that lived there. Water and air mages were more likely to move around and not settle down, a trait they probably got from the elements they had an affinity towards. In that sense, I was the complete opposite. My affinity was to mother earth, and I had a connection with all the things that grew on her, from tiny weeds to huge trees. Like the plants, I needed to feel settled down, to feel like I had roots in a place to be completely comfortable. I'd felt that in Ravenshire, but not in my parents' home.

Now here, in Mistvale, I was hopeful I'd feel that again, that sense of home I yearned for.

I shook off the lingering tension in my arms and jumped, grabbing hold of one of the lower branches of the oak tree before hauling myself up. Once I was there, I didn't stop. I kept climbing until I'd reached the last branch that would support my weight. From this height, I could see the whole cul-de-sac. The houses were in a rough circle, with the Silent Creek Park at my back, and I could see all the houses from here. Including Jai's. I could see him, too. He was just stepping out of his house with his dog, leash in hand. I'd stopped feeling like a stalker by now, completely accepting my status of being one, and I watched as Jai and his dog walked down the short driveway before turning toward my house.

I knew I should look away, but I kept watching as they walked. The dog tugged on the leash every few seconds, his head cocked to one side, while Jai walked at a slow, sedate pace. It was even slower than the pace he'd maintained the last time I'd seen him, and I wondered if he was feeling even worse. I wanted to check up on him. I wanted to hold his hand and figure out exactly what he was suffering with. The thing was, I had no clue how I could do that without coming off as a crazy guy or a weirdo. It wasn't like I could tell him I was a mage and it wasn't like I'd be able to help him, even if I knew what he was suffering from. I knew the way my magic had acted the other day had been nothing but a fluke, and there was no way I'd be able to help him. So why was I so obsessed with this man? Why couldn't I just let him go? And why had I turned into a stalker in my attempt to get to know more about him?

I swore as I watched the dog tug on his leash a bit too hard and escape Jai's hold. Jai looked stunned for a second as if he couldn't comprehend what had happened, but then he seemed to gather himself and chase the dog, though I knew he wasn't healthy enough to be doing that. I switched my gaze to the dog and watched it sneak into my neighbor's yard. I knew they had a dog. Seemed like Jai's doggo just wanted to make a friend.

I scrambled down the tree and raced to the front just as Jai appeared on the sidewalk. My sudden appearance startled him and he went down in the same spot I'd found him last time. I heard him curse as he went down and hurried to help him, pulling him upright. He swayed in my arms and I realized he was dizzy. Just like last time, my magic reacted without my urging and the amount of pain I sensed in him almost made me stagger. There were a few cuts on his palm from where he'd scraped them on the sidewalk and they had some blood on them, but the pain Jai felt was too much to be just from the scrapes. What the hell was going on with him?

"Come on, you need to sit," I said, leading him to my small porch. We were almost there when he froze suddenly, making us almost fall over since he'd been leaning against me.

"What's wrong?"

"Pads. My dog! I need to find him. Let me go." I tightened my grip around his waist as he tried to get away.

"Calm down, calm down. I saw him sneak into a neighbor's yard. How about you get seated here and I'll go get him, okay?"

Jai looked up at me with his brown eyes that reminded me of freshly turned soil, a sheen of wetness covering them. "You'll find him?"

"I promise. Just take a seat and I'll get him. His name is Pads?"

"Padfoot," Jai explained as he took a seat on the porch, his eyes snapping shut as if he was trying to fight another wave of dizziness.

"Alright, hold on. I'll be right back." I wanted to hold him for a minute and maybe try to reduce some of his pain, but I didn't know if my magic would be of any help. The best way I could help Jai right now was by getting his dog back. Then I'd patch up his wounds. I may not have the help of my magic, but I knew how to do basic first-aid. I wasn't completely useless, no matter what my parents had liked to tell me.

Jai

I kept my eyes shut as I took a few shallow breaths and tried to escape the dizziness. I knew my hands weren't hurt too badly, but my body apparently hadn't gotten the memo. It was the same every time. No matter how few drops I bled, my body always reacted like I was on the brink of death, making me dizzy and unsteady.

I couldn't believe I'd stumbled in front of Raphael. Again. On my knees. *Again.* If it wasn't so absolutely humiliating, it would be funny how I ended up on my knees every time I came across Raphael, but it was. It was so damn embarrassing. I wished the ground would open up and swallow me so I wouldn't have to face him again. Why did this keep happening?

He was leaps and bounds out of my league and I knew there was no way he'd want me. The least I could've done was maintain my distance. Maybe we could've even become friends for a short while before he realized how soul sucking being my friend was. Instead, I'd been taking every opportunity I could to humiliate myself in front of him. Fuck, I was pathetic.

A cheery woof broke me out of my self-deprecating thoughts and then Pads was there, covering my face with licks. My heart stuttered in my chest as relief swamped over me and I pulled him into my arms, holding on to his neck tightly as I let his familiar, furry body comfort me. Padfoot wasn't just my dog, he was my companion, my partner in crime and the only being in the world who wasn't tired of dealing with me. He didn't care if I couldn't take him on walks every day or if there were days where all I wanted to do was lie in bed and cuddle him. He didn't mind that I never went out, that I could almost never play with him. He was just there for me. I loved him, and even the thought of losing him was enough to make me panic.

I finally opened my eyes to see Raphael watching us with a soft smile on his face. My cheeks blazed hot as I gave him what I hoped was a grateful smile. "Thank you so much for finding him, Raphael."

"It was no problem. He was just socializing with the neighbor's dog. Also, call me Raph."

I nodded and bit my lip as I readied myself to stand up. I felt steady enough that I knew I wouldn't stumble. "Alright, then. I'll get out of your hair. Sorry for troubling you. Again."

Raphael's brows shot up to his hairline and he shook his head as he walked closer. "Oh no, you're not leaving yet. I need to clean up those scratches on your palms. God knows what nasty germs you picked up from the sidewalk. How about you come in and I'll patch you up over some tea and cookies?"

Tea and cookies? I almost chuckled because that had been my grandma's go to for every problem. Wow. I'd just compared my neighbor and, hopefully, potential-friend to my grandmother. Way to go, Jai.

Raphael was walking over to his door before I could decline his invitation. He held the door open and looked at me expectantly. With a sigh and a shake of my head, I grabbed Padfoot's leash and led him inside.

The floor plan of Raphael's house seemed similar to mine, but while I'd decorated my living room in soft browns, Raphael's was an explosion of beige and green. There were plants *everywhere*. It gave the room a cool, minty atmosphere and a strange sort of calm washed over me as I took a seat on his beige couch, which was half covered in pillows. Green pillows.

"First, I'll disinfect your wounds and then I'll make some tea, alright?"

I nodded as he walked into where I guessed the bathroom was and came back with a first aid kit. He kneeled on the floor in front of me, his blond hair falling into his face as he looked through the first aid kit. My fingers itched to tuck the strands behind his ear and I bit my lip to stop myself. What the fuck was wrong with me? He was a stranger, no matter how gorgeous or kind he was.

He tucked his hair behind his ear as he grabbed my palm lightly in his. The moment our skin touched, a strange zing ran through my body, followed immediately by a strange sense of calm. It seemed to wash over my body and I knew I was just imagining it, but I almost felt like the aches in my body became less intense as the feeling washed over me.

I shook my head to get rid of the weird feeling and focused on Raphael as he soaked a cotton ball into disinfectant and swiped it over my palm in careful, light strokes. I'd gotten so used to all kinds of medical treatments from so many people that his gentleness took me by surprise. The nurses weren't exactly harsh, but I was just another patient to them. Raphael, though, he treated my wounds as if he *cared*.

Nah, it was just fanciful thinking. Why the hell would Raphael care about me?

As he treated my hand, I realized I should probably tell him why he kept finding me on my knees on his sidewalk. Plus, nothing worked easier at pushing someone away than telling them you were terminally ill.

"Um, sorry I keep falling over at your place. I swear it isn't intentional. I have a rare heart illness which has also fucked up my lungs, so sometimes I get exhausted easily. Well, most of the time."

"It's okay, you don't need to explain yourself to me," Raphael said, shooting me a soft smile that lit up his unique eyes. I'd never seen eyes quite like his before. They were a mix and green and brown, but they were much darker than any green eyes I'd ever seen. If I had to compare, I'd say his eyes looked like tree bark coated in moss. It looked way more enchanting than it sounded.

It surprised me when he went back to covering the cuts with small bandaids, as if my confession meant nothing. Usually, when I told people about my illness, they had a million questions. *How long have you been sick? Is it terminal? What about treatments?* Yet, here he was, acting as if my illness was no big deal.

For the first time, a ray of hope filled me. Could I actually have a shot? Did I have a chance at making Raphael my friend?

"All done! Now, how about some tea? Or would you prefer coffee?"

"No caffeine, please. Tea sounds great." Caffeine didn't gel well with my medicines. If I was being honest, a lot of things didn't jam with me. Normal friendship was one of them. I had two best friends and one of them was my younger brother, while the other one was someone I only talked to online and had never actually met.

It wasn't that I hadn't tried. I had. So many times, I'd made friends only for them to slowly drift away after one too many canceled plans. Sooner or later, they realized I would never be there for them the way they had to be there for me. I'd never be able to go to a party with them, or a trip or even hang out for longer than an hour or two unless it was in the comfort of my own home. I didn't fault them for ditching me. I would've probably done the same if the roles were reversed. It still stung, though it had also taught me I wasn't made to have friends.

I had Padfoot and my brother, and they were enough. I needed them to be enough, or I knew I'd succumb to the depression that was always there, waiting for me to feel weak to pounce on me. As if I didn't already have enough problems to deal with.

"You okay?" Raphael asked as he placed a tray with two cups of tea, sugar, cream, and some cookies on the coffee table before me. I looked up at him and blinked, wondering if I was seeing things. There wasn't a squirrel on his shoulder, right?

"Is that a squirrel?" My voice was so soaked in disbelief and yet all Raph did was push the squirrel's bushy tail away from his face and grin at me.

"Oh yes, this is Neya. She lives here too. Well, she lives in the tree in my backyard, but she spends most of her time in here."

"You have a pet squirrel," I stated in a dry voice, still reluctant to believe what I was seeing and what he was telling me. They looked adorable together, to be honest. The squirrel—Neya—had wrapped herself around Raphael's neck and looked all kinds of comfy as she watched me with her beady black eyes.

He scrunched up his nose in a way that made him look adorable, and I realized he had some light freckles on his nose that seemed to make him even cuter. I needed to stop noticing how gorgeous he was.

"I wouldn't call her a pet, per se. She's more of a friend to me, honestly."

"Like me and Padfoot," I said with a smile as I grabbed my cup. I added some sugar, though milk was another no-no for me. I had a lot of those, too.

If someone were to take a peek into my thoughts, they would think I was the most whiny son of a bitch ever. But then again, it was better to whine where no one could hear me than to appear pathetic, right? Over the years, I'd gotten used to keeping my pain to myself, mostly because I hated the guilt that came with telling my parents about it and the way it had made me feel so much *less* when I was with my friends,

"Yep. You can let him go, you know. The backyard is secure, he won't go anywhere," Raphael said as he took a seat on a nearby armchair. I nodded and unclipped Padfoot's leash, but instead of going outside like I thought he would, he rushed to Raphael's side and started sniffing at Neya.

Raphael chuckled and petted Pads as he continued to sniff Neya. The tiny squirrel clung to Raph's ear for a minute before hesitantly reaching for Padfoot.

My sweet boy froze immediately, standing stock still as Neya hopped onto his back. He went a little cross-eyed trying to find the squirrel, but then he seemed to shrug and race off toward the backyard, Neya holding on to him for the ride.

"He wouldn't hurt her, right?" I wondered aloud. Padfoot was a sweet guy, but he was huge compared to Neya.

"Nah, I bet they'll already be friends by the time you leave."

I grinned at his pronouncement and went back to sipping my tea. The silence turned awkward quickly, since we were both still strangers. I looked around the room, trying to find something to talk about because I knew I'd start getting anxious if the awkwardness continued.

"You have a lot of plants," I blurted out, immediately cringing at my obvious statement.

Raphael didn't seem to mind, though. He just gave me this wide smile that lit up his dark eyes and nodded. "Yeah, I'm a nature lover. I bought this place because of the tree in the backyard. I like the greenery, I suppose."

I nodded as I peeked out the back door and a sound of surprise and awe slipped out of me as I spotted the humongous oak tree in his backyard. Damn, the tree was enormous. If I were healthy, I would've loved nothing more than to climb that tree. I used to do that when I was a kid, back before my condition turned so bad that even the slightest exertion tired me. I missed doing that. I missed doing a lot of things.

I shook off the thoughts with a practiced precision and focused on Raphael as he sipped his tea. The guy was gorgeous. I couldn't stop thinking about that. It wasn't just his physical attributes, either. He was a sweet guy. He'd helped me both the times he'd met me, and I'd never felt like I'd inconvenienced him, even though everyone—including my parents—made me feel so, albeit unintentionally. I hated how much I had to depend on others, and yet I didn't feel like that when he helped me. The way his presence always seemed to calm me down or reduce my exhaustion was something I couldn't figure out. Did I feel better because I enjoyed his company? That had to be it, right? After all, what else could it be?

"You live just a few houses away, right?" Raphael asked, pulling me out of my thoughts. I nodded, and he smiled before extending his hand, palm up. "Can I have your phone for a minute?"

My brows furrowed at the strange request, but I pulled my phone out of my pocket and handed it to him, curious about what he wanted it for.

He tapped a few keys before handing the phone back to me. "There. You have my number now. Call or text if you'd like to hangout sometime."

"You want to be my friend?" I asked, and the disbelief couldn't have been clearer in my voice.

Raphael shot me a wicked grin, winking as he got up, the empty tray in his hands. As he reached the doorway, he called out, disappearing into the kitchen mid-sentence so I couldn't tell if he truly meant it. "Friends would be a good place to start, don't you think?"

Wait, what?

THREE

Jai

The Farmer's Market was my one indulgence. The one place I shored up my energy to go to every second Sunday. The place wasn't huge, which was always a bonus, and though there were around twenty booths in all, I had a few favorites that I stuck to to minimize my exertion. The fresh produce here was to die for and the homemade bath salts and soaps from Nonna May's always helped with my sore muscles and aches, so there was that.

I loved living in Mistvale. It wasn't a huge town, but there were enough people that not everyone was in everyone else's business. Mistvale had an old, 1920s feel to it, and it was a mismatch of old and new buildings. Even though I'd lived here for my whole life, I had yet to see every part of it. I knew the market and the shopping center like the back of my hand, but other than that there were only a few places I'd been to yet, one of which was the hospital.

As I walked through the crowd, keeping a steady pace as I headed towards the Fruity foods booth, I wondered what

Raphael was up to. After he'd given me his number, I'd spent the past two days almost texting him before chickening out at the last moment. It wasn't that I didn't like him or that I wasn't interested in getting to know him better. It was just that I was scared. I was scared of hoping again. I was scared that if I spent more than a few minutes with him at a time, he'd realize how boring and fucked up I was and he'd give up like everyone else. Even though it had been awkward both times, I'd enjoyed talking to him. I didn't want my illness to steal another possible-friend from me like it always did. And the only way to make sure of that was to keep Raphael at a distance. Yet, my fingers itched to pull out my phone and send him a text. What if I texted him but didn't hang out with him? Could a friendship like that work? It worked with my online best friend Cassian. But then again, us meeting up was impossible unless preplanned, so it wasn't like I was intentionally avoiding him. It wouldn't be the same if I did that to Raphael, would it?

I shook my head as I bought some apples, trying my best to keep my mind blank. It was no use thinking about the what-ifs. I knew I'd break sooner or later. I would end up texting him and then we'd hang out a few times if I was lucky. Raphael would soon realize that there was no way we could be friends and then he'd disappear like every other friend before him did and I'd have to avoid him for as long as we were neighbors.

At least I wouldn't be so lonely for the next few days though, right? That had to count for something.

Raphael

It was not my fault. It was not my fault that the moment I stepped into the clearing that hosted the farmer's market my eyes strayed towards Jai and latched on to him as if I'd been looking for him. I have no clue how I spotted him the moment I arrived. It was as if some part of me was already in tune with him even though we barely knew each other.

He hadn't texted me. I wanted to believe it was because he was trying to build up the courage and not because he wasn't interested in getting together, but it could be either of the reasons. He'd been almost reluctant to talk to me. I'd thought it was because of his illness. I'd heard something in his voice when he told me about it, as if he expected me to make a big deal out of it. Luckily for me, I'd already known he was sick from our first meeting, so it had been easy to act like I didn't care. And I really didn't. At least, not in the sense he expected me to.

I didn't care that his illness would hinder him from hanging out with me but I did care that I couldn't heal him. If I wasn't so incompetent, I might have been able to heal him. Then again, I still didn't know the extent of it. If his illness was something he'd had since he was born or if it was some kind of defect in his organs, then it was possible even my parents wouldn't be able to heal him. The healing magic was strange. It could heal stab wounds to the heart but not illnesses like cancer.

I shook my head and startled to a stop as I realized I'd unconsciously started following Jai. What the hell was wrong with me? I was going to end up making the guy think I was some kind of stalker. I was a stalker, wasn't I? And even though I had no ill intent towards him, I didn't want him to think that of me. Not after he was already so unwilling to get to know me.

I turned around before he could spot me and headed towards my favorite herbs booth. The lady was a nice, old mage who grew herbs in her backyard. Not many mages lived out here in the human world, preferring to stay in Ravenshire. There were the nomads, of course and the adventure enthusiasts, but most of them preferred to live on the island. If it weren't for the way I was treated there, I'd have picked Ravenshire over Mistvale any day too. It wasn't that Mistvale wasn't beautiful in its own right, but it didn't come close to the magnificence that was Ravenshire. Plus, it didn't feel like home.

I was happy here, though. Even if it had been just two weeks and I kinda missed my sister—though it was clear she didn't miss me much, if at all. I felt much better about myself here than I ever had before. Hopefully, Mistvale would soon feel like home. As the lady rang up my purchases, I smiled to myself, knowing I'd be okay. I'd find a way to be happy. I wasn't lacking for money but I was still hoping to find some kind of job or something to take up my time. Since I'd discovered my ability to heal animals I was thinking about volunteering at some kind of animal shelter. If animals were all I could heal, then I'd put my powers to good use.

I came to a stop as I reached the exit and my eyes fell on Jai yet again. He was walking towards the parking lot, a few paper bags clutched in his hands. I'd walked here since the market wasn't far from home but I knew the distance was probably too much for Jai to walk, especially with all that extra weight. As I watched, Jai got on his knees, fishing around under the car. He must've dropped the keys, I realized even as my feet started taking me in his direction before I'd made a decision to approach him. Then again, I couldn't let the opportunity go, could I?

"We need to stop meeting like this, Jai," I said, amusement lacing every word.

Jai's head shot up, his eyes widening slightly as he swore under his breath. "We really do," he mumbled as he finally found his keys and got to his feet, dusting off his knees. "What are you doing here?"

I raised my hand so he could see the bag I was holding and rest assured that I wasn't stalking him. I really wasn't. "Getting some herbs for my teas. What about you?"

"Just some groceries and stuff." He got a thoughtful look on his face as he eyed the bag in my hand before looking up at me, "Was the tea you made that day herbal too? Because after I left your house, I felt way less tired than I should've, especially after getting hurt."

My brows furrowed as I tried to remember the tea I'd made him two days ago. It had been ginger and honey, nothing special so why would—

My thoughts screeched to a halt. It couldn't be, could it? My magic didn't work on humans or mages. It couldn't be possible that it worked on him when it had never worked on anyone else, right? But what other reason could there be? It could've been a coincidence but I didn't believe in coincidences. But it *couldn't* be my magic. My magic was weak and useless. It was *nothing*. How could it have helped him?

Only one way to figure it out.

"It was, actually. I'm glad it helped. If you ever need more of it, come by whenever. I'd be happy to make it for you."

"Or you could just give me the ingredients," he offered and I almost rolled my eyes at him but opted to wink instead.

"Nah, how would I lure you back then? At least if you wanted the tea, you would drop by sometime."

Jai looked away, biting his lower lip as he did. His skin was a nice tan color and looked almost golden under the slight sunshine. Even without the red staining his cheeks, I could tell he was blushing by the way he averted his eyes.

"Oh, can you give me a lift? I could walk back, but really, how would you feel watching me trudge along the path while you drove in your car with the air conditioner on?"

Jai chuckled lightly as he shook his head, but my joke made him look back up at me. I shot him a smile as he opened the passenger side door and waved me inside. "So gentlemanly," I couldn't help quipping as he shut the door and he rolled his eyes at me again before putting the bags in the trunk and climbing inside.

"So what do you say about coming over to mine so I can make you some tea? Maybe we could watch a movie or something? Only if you want to, though," I added as I remembered the fact that he hadn't texted me. Maybe I should take the hint and back off. Maybe his reluctance had nothing to do with him and everything to do with me. Maybe he simply wasn't interested and I was being a jerk trying to hang on to him.

"I'll need to drop the groceries at home and let Padfoot out first," Jai said as he started the car and I breathed out a sigh of relief as butterflies fluttered in my belly. It had been so long since I'd just hung out with someone without wondering if they really liked me or if they were just waiting for a chance to bully me about my powers. Hell, I couldn't even remember the last time I'd dated someone, much less gone on a date. Not that this was a date, of course.

"You can bring Padfoot with us, if you want. He can play in the backyard."

Jai shot me a wide smile, making me realize yet again that he was really close to Padfoot. The way he'd panicked the other day when he'd escaped had told me as much.

"You really love Padfoot, don't you?" I mused aloud and Jai smiled somewhat sadly as he stared out the front.

"Yeah. He's the only one who never gets tired of me. Sooner or later, everyone does, but he has stuck with me for three years now and he loves me just as much as he did in the beginning." He almost sounded like he was warning me that I'd get tired of him. If he was, he was about to be very surprised. I'd lived under the thumbs of bullies for more than a century. I had a well of patience and I'd be only too happy to use it for someone like Jai. It hadn't been long since we met, but even so I already felt more at ease with him than I had with anyone other than my sister for my whole life. There was something about Jai that called to me on a deeper level.

If what he'd said was true, he needed my powers to feel better and I needed his presence. It seemed like we could have the perfect deal. If I could prove for certain that my powers really did work on him, that it hadn't just been a fluke, or wishful thinking. I remembered the way my magic had rushed towards him the two times I'd touched him. That, along with what Jai had said was enough to light up that old hope in me, the hope that I wasn't completely useless and that my magic could be good for something. I just hoped it wouldn't be another red herring. I was really tired of hoping for things that never came to be.

FOUR

Raphael

I was still a teensy bit surprised that Jai agreed to hang out with me. I'd expected to have to ask him at least a few times, maybe even beg him in the end. My thoughts had started to head down that old road of self-loathing before he said yes, and I knew that if he'd said no, I wouldn't have pushed. I probably would've avoided him as much as I could in the future, but he'd said yes and now here we were. Now, if only I could figure out if I could really help him...

Jai unclipped Padfoot's leash as I slid the back door open, and Padfoot shot out into the backyard. Before I could turn away, Neya scurried inside and scampered up my body, nuzzling into my cheek once she reached my shoulder. "Hello, little miss," I greeted her.

Jai's chuckle made me turn to look at him. He was watching me with a smile on his face. Damn, he was such a fine sight. With his square, black-rimmed glasses and his dark hair that was all over the place, he looked more like a runway model than not. "What?" I asked him when I realized he was still watching me.

Jai shook his head, his smile still in place. "Nothing. I was just appreciating how sweet you are with her. I believe that the best way to figure a person out is to see how they act with animals."

"Me too!" I exclaimed, glad I wasn't the only one who did that. It was a pretty sound theory, both for a mage and a human. If a mage treated his semlee as well as other animals with the same amount of kindness, he would be a good man. If a mage only cared for his semlee, I'd stay far away from him. "The way you were worried about Padfoot the other day was all I needed to see to know you're as sweet as you look."

Jai smiled at me and for a minute we just started at each other with wide smiles on our faces. Neya nipped at my ear, reminding me that I had things to do. I hoped Jai couldn't see the blush that I was sure was on my face as I waved towards the TV. "Why don't you find something to watch? I love everything except classics." It wasn't that I didn't enjoy classic movies, it was just that I'd done a Hollywood stint some sixty years ago—it was my own way of acting out and going against my parents—and though my hair had been short and brown back then, I was pretty sure Jai could recognize me if he was sitting right next to me while we watched it. I'd enjoyed working in the movie industry, even if everyone from Ravenshire had used it as just another reason to hate me. Obviously I had to leave after a few years before people got suspicious. I was still on some of the weird celebrity disappearances lists. The people of Ravenshire didn't do shit like that, because secrecy was very important to them. I understood the need for secrecy and I probably wouldn't have done it now—especially since the arrival of social media changed everything—but back then, I'd tried all kinds of things in an attempt to get my parents to like me. Look how that worked out.

I walked into the kitchen as Jai fiddled with the remote and pulled out my kettle, filling it with water and herbs before setting it on the stove. I'd decided to go easy with some basil leaves and ginger for the tea, since I knew my tea was *not* magical. Now, how to go about touching Jai without looking like a pervert or an asshole? I couldn't be sure if my magic had helped him unless I used it on him again and I couldn't do *that* without touching him. Such a dilemma.

I puzzled over it as I strained the tea into a porcelain kettle I'd bought from a tiny clay shop in town. I hadn't actually expected to use it. I'd just bought it because of the pretty design on it. Placing two matching teacups on the tray, along with sugar—since neither of us took cream, as I'd realized last time—and the kettle, I carried the whole thing into the living room where Jai was stretching his arms above his head with a pained groan. He straightened up as soon as he saw me and shot me an embarrassed smile. "Sorry, my muscles get stiff really easily."

"Nothing to apologize for," I said with a shake of my head while wondering who the fuck made him think he ever had to apologize for his own discomfort. Though it did give me an idea of how I could touch him and I smiled as I placed the tray on the coffee table before taking a seat on the other end of the couch.

"Hey, by the way, I know this massage technique that might help with the pain. Would you like me to try?"

Jai shot me an amused smile as he hit play on the movie he'd picked—an action flick that I'd already watched and enjoyed once—before saying, "You know I'm not a guinea pig, right?"

It took me a moment to realize what he was saying and my eyes widened in horror. Shit. He must get that all the time, right? I'd seen it enough at the hospitals when I accompanied my parents. People always had a recommendation, something that was guaranteed to help. I'd always wondered how people with zero medical background could think they knew exactly what to do. I hated the way they treated the person who was ill, like a guinea pig to experiment on as they pleased. Now here I was doing the same thing.

"Fuck, I'm so sorry. I didn't mean to offend you, I swear. I didn't think how it would sound, I just didn't want you to be in pain if I could do something about it. I'm so so-" Jai's finger on my lips effectively cut me off and I went a bit cross-eyed as I tried to look at his finger before meeting his eyes.

He was grinning at me, his brown eyes dancing with humor behind his glasses. He didn't remove his finger as he spoke and I found myself wishing I could kiss it. "It's okay, Raph. I was just teasing you. I'd never turn down a free massage. If I could afford it, I'd hire a live-in masseuse to give me massages at all times."

"I'll do it for free. Where do I apply?" I mumbled against his finger and he chuckled before pulling away, shaking his head as he grinned at me even though I was being completely serious.

"Alright. Drink your tea, watch the movie and enjoy my supremely awesome shoulder massage," I told him as I stood up and walked around the couch so I was standing behind him. I placed my palms flat against his shoulders, digging my fingers into the skin lightly before moving upwards. I let the tiniest bit of my magic flow through my palms and into him, keeping it low enough that he wouldn't sense it. Even though humans didn't know about magic, they could sense it most of the time, especially when they were in close proximity to it. Or at least, that's what my mother had told me back when she still had hopes for me.

I kept up a steady rhythm, running my palms all the way to his shoulder blades and letting more of my magic seep through. I didn't actually know how to give a professional massage and I also had no clue how to get my magic to work, but it was flowing through my palms into Jai in a steady rhythm and I hoped it was doing something, because if it was, then it would mean that my magic wasn't useless. If Jai was the only person I'd ever be able to help with my magic then I'd be perfectly content.

Jai hummed deep in his throat and the sound did something to me, making butterflies flutter in my stomach. The sound made me wonder how it'd feel if he made that sound with his lips on mine. Or somewhere else on my body. I started speaking to get the thoughts out of my head before my body reacted and gave me away, "Feel good?"

Jai tested my control by humming again and it sounded so much like a moan that I had to bite my lip really hard to stop my brain from creating all these scenarios in my head. Damn, why the hell was he so fucking sexy? How was I supposed to give him a nice, innocent massage when he kept making all these dirty sounds? The fun fact was I knew without a doubt he had absolutely no clue how absolutely hot he sounded.

To save the last of my sanity, I pushed a little more of my magic into him before pulling away. All I wanted to do was lean forward and press my lips to the nape of his neck but I made myself walk over to my side of the couch and resume my seat. Jai had his eyes closed, a smile tilting his soft lips, his glasses sitting at the tip of his nose as if they were ready to take the plunge at any moment. My eyes roamed over his face, taking in his subliminal beauty. He wasn't the kind of guy I was usually attracted to. He was lean—too thin, to be honest, but I was sure that had more to do with his illness than his eating habits—and kinda short. With his glasses and soft smile, he looked nerdy and adorable. The men I hooked up with were usually big, muscular gym buffs. Yet, here I was, fantasizing about kissing him and doing a lot more dirty things with him. Friends, we were supposed to be friends.

His eyes snapped open and I froze as our gazes locked, wondering for a second if he'd read my thoughts and if so, what did he think? It took me only another few seconds to realize I was being an idiot and I flushed under his unwavering gaze, making him arch a brow at me. I'd die before I told him what I'd been thinking about.

"So, did it work?"

"You have magic hands," he declared and I bit back my gasp as I realized that he meant it as a compliment rather than an observation. Thank mother for that.

I smiled at him, feeling a bit bashful even as I realized what this meant. Somehow, my magic had taken his pain away. My magic that worked on no other human had worked on Jai. What was so special about him? I could sense that he was a hundred percent human. So was he special to me specifically? And if so, why? Why was my magic connected to him?

Jai

I'd forgotten how good it felt to just hang out with someone else. To just sit with a friend and watch a movie while you traded comments and opinions on it. Add to it the fact that Raphael's massage had magically gotten rid of most of the aches that plagued me twenty-four-seven and I was practically in heaven.

I knew it must've been the tea that did most of the work, but the massage had felt pretty damn good too. Raph's hands had been soft and yet firm on my skin as he kneaded my stiff muscles and I hadn't been able to stop myself from expressing my pleasure, even though it had been a tad embarrassing.

When the movie ended, I found myself wishing I could stay for longer and the thought surprised me. Usually, I was eager to go home whenever I was out because staying at home was always the least painful option. But now, without the pain to hinder me, all I wanted to do was sit with Raphael and watch more movies. I didn't want to seem clingy though, so I got to my feet as I called out for Padfoot, who had fallen asleep on the deck outside.

"Thank you for having me over. I enjoyed spending time with you."

"I had fun too. We should do this again. You can call or text if you'd like to employ my free massage services again," Raphael joked as I clipped Padfoot's leash back on.

I chuckled as I straightened up, shaking my head. "Nah, I'll pay you. How does a home-cooked dinner sound for a fair payment?" I offered. Staying at home all day meant I was pretty good at all the homey things, including cooking.

"Ooh, that sounds perfect! I'll be looking forward to this dinner." Raphael's voice told me he really would enjoy the meal and that made me all the happier to cook for him.

As I walked the three blocks to my house, I mulled over how much better I felt after spending a whole morning out and about. Sure, hanging out with Raphael had been mostly relaxing but sometimes even that tired me out. Today had been a good day.

Once I was home, I changed into my pajamas even though it was barely lunchtime. It wasn't as if I needed to go out again, so I might as well be comfy, right?

Pads lumbered around the living room for a moment before jumping up on the couch and deciding to take a nap. It was what he usually did while I cooked lunch. I put my playlist on and connected the bluetooth speaker before making myself a nice sandwich.

Once I was done eating, I grabbed the book I'd been reading and snuggled up with Pads on the couch, resting half of my body on him because he was huge and I loved him. He was a husky my father had bought me after I'd had a particularly bad month and he was my life. He gave my cheek a welcoming lick before snuffling against my ear and making me giggle. "Stop it," I complained, swatting him lightly. He woofed in a way that told me he was laughing before going back to sleep.

My phone pinged before I could start reading and I smiled when I saw a text from Cassian. He was my closest friend, even though we'd never met and probably never would. Not because we couldn't or were too far away, but because we'd decided that together when we first started talking. I knew that if we met, I'd slowly lose him too, so it was better to stay like this. He seemed to have reasons of his own to stay away, so it worked perfectly for us.

Cass: Yo, Jai. Do you believe in magic?

It wasn't the first time he'd texted me a random, completely out of nowhere question, and usually my answers were just as quick and flippant. But today, for some reason, I found myself giving his questions an actual thought as I answered him.

Jai: Hmmm…That's a tough one. My fav genre to read is fantasy. I love magic. I love the idea of nature or elements giving you the power to do good. I love the idea of something more existing in the world. But would I believe someone if they told me they could do magic?

Cass: Would you?

Jai: I guess that depends on whether they could prove it. If someone gave me solid proof they could do magic, then there's no reason I wouldn't believe them. I might need some time to come to terms with it, of course. We all know us humans are very stuck in our ways. I'd like to believe that I can change, though.

Cass: Good. I'd believe it too, ya know. I mean, we can't be the only species of the 'homo sapiens' class, right? (Is it a class, BTW?) I mean, there are so many sub-species of so many creatures, why not humans?

Jai: I love how you just mixed fantasy with science and made it all sound so fucking reasonable. This is why you're my best friend.

Cass: Nah, it's because of my awesome good looks and my charming nature.

Jai: Pfft. Right. I have a magical world waiting for me to get back to. Talk later?

Cass: Sure. Give my love to Pads.

Jai: Give April a hug from me.

Cass: Ha ha ha.

I grinned as I locked my phone, imagining Cassian trying to hug his huge bird. I didn't know how he got her or if it was even legal to have her as a pet, but Cassian was the proud daddy of a huge eagle-owl named April. She was huge but a complete sweetheart, as far as I could tell, despite her fire red eyes and sharp talons. (I've seen way too many pictures of her because we're both dedicated pet-pics swappers.)

I turned back to my book, sinking further into Padfoot's fur as I delved back into a magical world. I didn't know if magic really existed, but between the pages of my books, I knew I'd always find it.

FIVE

Raphael

Even though Jai told me he'd invite me to dinner, I hadn't really been expecting it when he called me two days later asking if I was free to have dinner with him. I'd said yes instantly, of course, and now I was staring at my closet trying to figure out what to wear. I had to remind myself that it wasn't a date as I picked a soft cashmere sweater that my sister had gifted me last Christmas. She'd said the color matched my eyes and I loved the soft wool. I paired it with faded blue jeans and my trusty sneakers before checking my appearance in the mirror. I ran a comb through my hair, removing the tangles and the twigs that had somehow ended up in there—hmm, maybe when I'd been climbing the tree earlier? I hated hair products, because they always made my hair sticky no matter how many of them said they were non-sticky in big, bright letters. So once my hair was all brushed, I headed for the living room. I grabbed my keys and phone off the kitchen counter on my way.

Just as I opened the front door, Neya clambered up my leg, settling down on my shoulder like she planned on accompanying me.

"Oh, you're coming with me, are you?"

An image of Padfoot popped in my head and I chuckled. "You want to play with Padfoot, huh?"

I had one foot out the door when realization struck and I pulled back closing the door and turning my head to stare at Neya with wide eyes, my heart thumping in my chest as hope filled me. "Am I going crazy or did you just communicate with me?"

Neya nodded her tiny squirrel head as if she could understand exactly what I was saying and I gasped, awe and adoration filling me up. Every mage had a semlee, an animal they met during their youth who bonded with them and lived as long as they did, acting like their support system, their energy bank and all around companion. I'd never found mine. It had been just another thing that showed everyone I was a useless mage.

"Are you my familiar, Neya?" I whispered, afraid that if I said it any louder I'd realize that it had all been my imagination and Neya was just an ordinary squirrel.

Neya curled her whole body around my neck and a feeling of deep comfort enveloped me. She was hugging me, I realized. She was telling me that she was here, promising me that she'd always be here. She couldn't speak, not in the human way, but I could understand her perfectly. She shifted around a bit before nipping lightly at my neck. I expected to feel the sting, but instead I felt something snap into place, connecting the two of us for as long as we lived. Our bond was beautiful, a bright green thread of magic—the same color my healing magic manifested in—connecting my heart to hers.

I brought my palm up to her and she hopped onto it. Bringing her closer to my face, I kissed the top of her head before smiling at her, "Thank you so much for bonding with me, my sweet semlee. I promise to always care for you and protect you."

Neya dipped her head in acceptance before an image of Jai flashed into my mind, making me chuckle. "I didn't realize a semlee's duty included making sure their bonded followed their schedules," I joked, earning a nip to the tip of my thumb from my sassy semlee. She scrambled up my arm and I laughed as I finally headed out, my heart full of a newfound warmth at finally having my semlee with me. As much as I'd loved Raveshire, I was quickly discovering more and more things that connected me to Mistvale, one of them being the man I was headed to meet.

Jai

As I waited for Raph to get here, I wondered for the hundredth time if I'd been too hasty in inviting him over. I didn't want him to think I was desperate or needy, even though I kind of was. I'd really enjoyed hanging out with him the other day and I missed doing that, hanging out with someone else and just having fun. I really hoped Raphael wouldn't think I was too needy, because I didn't want to lose him so quickly. I didn't want him to realize how much work being my friend required or how one-sided things became with me after a while. I didn't think I could go through all of that again.

My phone pinged with an incoming text and I picked it off the counter, panicking at the thought that it might be Raph canceling our plans. My racing heart calmed down a bit when I saw it was my mom and I clicked the text open.

Ma: Don't forget. It's check-up day tomorrow. I'll pick you up at 9. Be ready. Love you.

Me: Love you too, Ma. I'll be ready. See ya.

I'd almost forgotten that it was time for my monthly hospital visit. Usually, I knew the day was coming a week in advance, but meeting Raph had thrown everything else out of whack in my mind. I knew I was getting too invested too soon—again—and I knew I would probably go back to being alone soon enough, just like I always did. Yet, I couldn't bring myself to not hope, to stay away from Raph so I wouldn't face the disappointment again. Spending time with Raph made me feel less alone and I'd take it even if there was a high chance he'd leave soon like everyone else did.

The knock on the door pulled me away from the memories of my past friends that had started to gather over me like storm clouds and I headed into the living room. I was smiling even before I opened the door. Raphael looked as gorgeous as he'd looked the few times we'd met. His blond hair hung in soft waves around his face and it seemed so silky my fingers itched to touch it. He wore a sweater that matched perfectly with the brown in his eyes and his easy smile had my smile growing wider as I waved him inside.

It was only once I'd closed the door that I realized Neya sat on Raphael's shoulder, looking all prim and proper with her tail wrapped around his neck. I'd seen a few squirrels in my backyard, but I'd never seen one who was so willing to stay close to humans, much less become someone's pet. Neya was a strange one.

The moment my eyes met hers, she scrambled down Raphael's body and climbed up mine, curling around my neck as I chuckled. I ran my fingertip lightly over her head, hoping not to scare her as I met Raph's eyes. "Seems like she likes me,"

I said and immediately jinxed myself because the next second Neya bit me, her tiny teeth sinking into the nape of my neck. "Ow!"

"What's wrong?" Raphael asked as Neya scampered back to him, acting like she hadn't just bitten me.

"I spoke too soon. She bit me," I told him, rubbing at my neck and wondering if I'd need rabies shots or something.

"Let me see," Raphael said as he leaned over to look at my neck. I sucked in a breath because all of a sudden he was in my space and so close. Gasping in a breath hadn't been the best idea though, because his scent filled my lungs, a minty-grassy scent that reminded me of trees and the Silent Creek Park. I'd been there just once, but I'd always remember the scent of the crisp air, full of the fragrance of the various plants that grew there. That's how Raph smelled, woodsy and grassy and all kind of delicious. I found myself leaning into him so the scent would envelope me too and I'm not sure what I would've done if the sound of Padfoot's bark hadn't pulled me out of the moment.

I scrambled back a step and realized Raphael had been watching me silently while I'd basically sniffed him like he was a bouquet of flowers—he smelled much better than that, but I digress. He smiled at me, his green-brown eyes alight with humor before winking. "It's okay, she didn't break your skin. No need to worry."

It took me a moment to realize what he was talking about and I shook my head to get rid of the thoughts plaguing my head. What would his lips taste like? Would they be all soft and sweet or tinged with a hint of spice after he had dinner? Would I get to taste them?

I thought about what he'd told me the other day, that starting as friends was a good idea. Had he really meant that?

And if so, could I be brave enough? Could I try, even though I knew sooner or later he'd leave?

It was what had always held me back from trying anything romantic. I was a lover of happily ever afters and I knew there was no scenario where I could have one. I knew I'd never live a full life. I might never even reach my thirties. If I fell in love, there would be only two things that could happen: either the one I fell in love with would leave me when he realized I was full of troubles or I'd die and leave him alone with a broken heart. Neither options appealed to me, and so I'd never tried pursuing anyone, not that I'd had a lot of occasions to. I was a homebody through and through.

But now, as I watched Raphael smiling as he petted Padfoot, for the first time in my life I wanted to try. I wanted to experience what it felt like to have a partner. What it felt like to kiss someone. What it felt like to give a part of myself to someone else, to share myself with them, body and soul. What I wanted more than anything, though, was to share it all with Raphael. Because he'd met me when I wasn't feeling all that great twice and yet he'd wanted to get to know me, not my illness. That's what made me want him, to want to try. I just hoped it wouldn't come back to bite me in the ass later.

Raphael

Even though the vegetable lasagna Jai had made looked absolutely delicious, I barely tasted it. My thoughts were running at the speed of a bullet, trying to come to terms with what had happened. Jai had no clue and he was a *human*. How was this even possible?

The moment Neya had bitten Jai flashed through my mind again, followed by the thought she'd sent me. *Semnyar.* Jai was my mate. After spending a century and a half alone, I'd found my semlee and my semnyar in the same day. Well, I'd met Jai a few days ago and Neya even before that, but now I knew just how important they both were. I was pretty sure I was in shock and would be freaking out as soon as it all filtered through. Jai was my semnyar, my other half. Wow. I'd never expected that.

Is that why my magic worked on him, then? Because our souls were connected? Or was it that my magic was just different from everyone else's?

I realized I'd already cleaned up my plate and looked up to see Jai staring off into nowhere, lost in his own thoughts. What was he thinking about? There was no way he knew about our bond, right? Of course, he didn't. He was a human.

Even though we were semnyars, our bond was still temporary, breakable. It would take work to make our bond stronger. We'd need to get to know each other better, spend time together. It was exactly like falling in love with someone, except the bond we made would last forever. Did that mean Jai would get my immortality? Fate wouldn't have made him my semnyar if he couldn't spend forever with me, right?

"You okay?" I asked, deciding I needed to stop thinking for now because I'd just keep going around in circles if I did.

Jai met my eyes but it took him a moment to come back from whatever thoughts he'd been lost in. He smiled at me, though it looked a bit forced. "Yeah, I'm okay. Would you like a second helping?"

"Nah, I'm full. This was delicious. I completely forgot to tell you that I don't eat meat but it seems you made vegetarian food anyway."

Jai smiled at me as he gathered our plates and I followed him into the kitchen. I wanted to spend every moment with him because I wasn't sure if he'd accept me as his semnyar. Shit, what would I do if he rejected me? Or if he didn't want me at all? He was human. Did he feel the pull of the bond like I did? Or did he have no clue that we were connected in the deepest possible way?

"I'm half-Indian. My mom's a strict Brahmin. That's a caste in Indian culture. Anyway, she doesn't eat meat and I guess I followed her lead when I was younger and now I can't stomach it at all. Dad tried to feed chicken to me a few times, but I didn't really like it." His scrunched up nose made him look absolutely adorable and I wanted nothing more than to lean forward and kiss him. I balled my hands into fists at my side to keep from touching him as I chuckled.

"Yeah, I'm not a fan of eating meat either, though I don't find many people who share my opinion."

"You found me," Jai said and wasn't that the truth? Just when I'd started feeling like I had no one, that I would never be enough for anyone, I'd found him. I'd found the one meant for me and I planned to make him see it.

"Yeah, yeah I did." My voice was soft and I knew I was smiling too widely but I couldn't help the warm feeling that rushed through me. I'd show him that I really wanted him and I'd make him realize we could be good together. I had to.

Once Jai had washed the dishes and I'd dried them—much to his annoyance since he was *completely capable of drying his own dishes*—I headed towards the front door, making my unwilling feet walk the few steps to it. I didn't want to leave, at least not without knowing when I'd next see him. Neya raced to me from wherever she'd been hanging out and settled on my shoulder.

"Thank you for dinner. It was delicious."

"My pleasure," Jai said with a smile, shuffling on his feet. He opened his mouth as if he wanted to say something before snapping it shut. Neya nipped at me, telling me to ask him already. I took a deep breath just as Jai opened his mouth again and then we both spoke up at the same time:

"Will you go out on a date with me?"

"Can I ask you out on a date?"

I met Jai's eyes and grinned sheepishly, running my fingers through my hair for something to do. "Should I consider that a yes, then?"

Jai bit his lip as he nodded before shuffling closer. He pulled my free hand into his, holding it palm up as he traced the lines on my palm with his finger. He kept his eyes trained on what he was doing as he spoke and I realized he felt uncomfortable about whatever he was about to say.

"You should know though, that I am a lot of work. I get tired super easily and some days I'm so tired I don't even want to get out of bed. I work from home and there are days I wouldn't leave the house for anything. I can't go out to clubs and parties and anything too exciting because my body can't handle the stress. I'm not trying to scare you off, or maybe I am, I don't know, but I want you to know. Every time I've tried being friends with anyone, they disappear after a while because they can't handle me. I...I like you, Raph and I don't want that to happen to us."

I let him talk because I knew he'd want to have said the words, to know that he'd warned me even though there was no way I'd abandon him, semnyar or not. He was such a sweet and gentle guy, I couldn't imagine how anyone had had the guts to give up on him.

I pulled his chin up so he was looking at me and so he'd see the sincerity in my eyes as I said, "I like you too, Jai. It doesn't matter if we spend all our dates right here in this room watching movies or reading books together or playing with our fur-babies. As long as we're spending time together, I'd be the happiest man ever. I know you need a lot of things that others might not, but I don't care. Honestly. I like you and I really want to try." *And you're my semnyar and I'd never, ever leave you,* I added silently. Soon, though. Soon I'd find the courage to tell him what I was and who he was to me. Thank god Ravenshire laws didn't forbid me from telling him everything. Semnyar bonds were the most sacred thing in the mage community, and there were no restrictions against telling your semnyar anything and everything about the magical world on the off-chance they belong to the non-magical world like Jai did.

"I want to try too," Jai whispered softly, his eyes bright with this quiet joy that had me leaning down and pressing a kiss on his cheek.

"How about tomorrow night? Can we have a date then?" I asked, trying—and failing, I'm sure—not to sound too eager.

Jai smiled before it fell away and a frown took its place. He bit his lip, taking a step back as he dropped his gaze so he was staring somewhere near my chest as he spoke, "I have a doctor's appointment tomorrow. Nothing's wrong, it's a monthly check-up. There are a lot of tests though, and they leave me exhausted. Maybe the day after tomorrow?"

His voice was so soft, so low as if he expected me to say no just because of that. What kind of people had he been friends with? Who would ever make someone feel guilty for worrying about their own health over someone else's entertainment?

"Perfect. Can I text you tomorrow, though? I'd like to make sure you're okay."

Jai looked up at me then, as if surprised I'd agreed so easily. As I watched him, a smile spread across his lips, making my heart skip a beat. Damn, he was beautiful when he smiled. "Of course you can. I'd...I'd like to hear from you," he admitted and I smiled at him as I pressed a kiss on his forehead before backing away before I lost myself too much in his silky soft skin and his warm scent. He smelled like...chocolate, actually. It was a strange scent to be on someone, but it seemed absolutely decadent to me since it was unique to Jai.

"I'll see you Friday, then."

Jai nodded, the smile still on his lips as I opened the door. I didn't want to leave, but I couldn't wait for Friday either. I had a date with my semnyar. Time to plan something that would sweep him off his feet without exhausting him. Challenge accepted.

SIX

Jai

Nine in the morning found me on my porch the next day, waiting for my mother to come pick me up. It was a routine we'd perfected over the last year since I finally decided that I wanted to live alone. It wasn't that I didn't love my family, it was just that I'd known that as long as I lived with them, they'd always be more focused on my illness than me.

I couldn't fault them for it either. I'd been born with a rare heart condition that had greatly reduced my survival chances and my parents had spent the first five years of my life desperately trying to do everything they could to keep me alive. I respected and loved them for that a lot. I couldn't imagine what they'd suffered through. My own childhood experiences had been pretty shitty, but I couldn't even fathom what I'd do if something like that happened to Padfoot, much less a child of my own.

Since I'd always lived with my illness, I didn't know all the technicalities of it. I only knew what it was called—Ventricular Septal Defect—and that too only because I'd googled it a few years ago. When it had been first discussed, I'd been too young to understand and now I only remembered what my paediatrics cardiologist had explained to me when I was in my early teens. In simple words, where a normal human heart had four separate chambers, my damaged one had an opening between the two ventricles, which made it so my oxygenated and deoxygenated blood kept mixing up, making my heart beat and work faster to make up for it. It also led to me being under oxygenated and that led to the plethora of other symptoms I carried.

When I was a kid, heart transplants were very expensive and they didn't always work. And now, after twenty three years of living with a heart like that, my lungs had also suffered some damage which made it hard for me to take deep breaths, since my heart and lungs were squashed together and putting pressure on each other. Which meant that though heart transplant was possible, I'd now also need new lungs because my heart had messed them up.

A year ago, my doctor had told me that I needed to look into organ transplant, but the problem was a) I'd need a donor who could donate both lungs and heart and b) even if I got a transplant, it would cost a shit ton of money and even then there would be no guarantee that I'd live more than five years if I survived for even that. In the end, I'd put off the decision because I felt pretty steady at the moment and I was scared. I was scared of dying on a surgery table. I wasn't afraid of death. I'd had a long time to come to terms with it, but if I had to die, I'd rather do it on my own terms.

The honk of my mom's car pulled me out of my thoughts that had turned way too dark for such a pretty morning and I gave myself a mental shake, pasting a smile on my face as I walked down the three steps and the short driveway to the car.

I felt pretty good today since I'd slept like a baby last night. Usually, some ache or pain kept me up until the wee hours of the morning but last night I'd fallen asleep the moment my head hit the pillow. I felt refreshed and like I could do anything. I didn't want to go to the hospital today because I knew the visit would suck every drop of energy out of me but it was a necessary evil. The tests were needed to make sure my heart wasn't about to die on me and I also needed to fill up my prescriptions.

"Hey, ma," I greeted her as I slid into the passenger seat. She immediately pulled me in a hug as if she hadn't seen me in years when I'd just been home for dinner a few days ago.

"Hey, beta. Are you okay?" She asked as soon as she pulled away, her brown eyes—the same color as mine—roaming all over me. My mom was beautiful in an understated kind of way. Her long, black hair was tied in a braid down her back, a red *bindi* on her forehead. Even though she'd moved to the US thirty years ago when she married my dad, she still carried some of her Indian traditions with her. She wore a long shirt and jeans, her hands as full of bangles as ever. My mom was pretty overbearing most of the time, but there had never been a moment that I hadn't known she loved me just as much as I loved her.

"I'm okay, Ma. Actually, I feel really good."

Ma smiled as she looked me over, her brown eyes lighting up as if she could actually see just how well I felt, "I can see that. What's that about?"

"Yeah, bhai, what's that about?" A voice piped up from the backseat and my head snapped around so fast I made my neck hurt.

Joy, my younger brother—I know, right? Jai and Joy. My parents sucked at the whole naming kids thing—sat in the backseat, watching me with mischief in his eyes. He was seventeen, and looked nothing like me. He had blond hair and light blue eyes like our dad, but his smile? That was all mom. The two of us were really close, despite the five years age difference. Many times I'd felt like he was the only one I could complain to about things without feeling guilty. He was my confidante and my best friend.

"Joy? What are you doing here? Don't you have school?"

His smile dimmed a bit as he looked away, chewing his lower lip as he met my eyes again. He shrugged. "I missed you. I didn't get to see you when you came over for dinner the other day and you never come by otherwise anymore."

Fuck. Here I was calling him my best friend and I hadn't even done that properly. Shit.

"How about you come by this weekend to play some video games? Pads misses you too."

Joy brightened immediately and we spent the rest of the drive listening to stories from his school. I'd missed this, I realized. As much as I liked standing on my own two feet, I missed my family too. I needed to be better at showing them that. God knew how much time I had left to do that.

***

After spending two hours going through the usual tests, I was ready to go home. I'd had my blood drawn, which always made me dizzy and since there hadn't been a bed available, I'd almost blacked out. My body didn't handle the loss of blood well, even if it was just a tiny vial-full.

I sat in my cardiologist's office, hoping I was a kid again so my mom could do the talking because I was so fucking tired. I just wanted my bed and my doggo. God, I turned into a whiny kid when I felt tired, didn't I?

"So, Jai, I'm impressed. Have you started a new diet or something?" Dr. Merryweather asked, his eyes never leaving my reports as he spoke.

"Huh? No, not really. Why?"

"Well, this is probably the first time in years, but I see some improvements in your reports. Your blood oxygen level has gone up by four percent and your blood pressure also seems to have gone down a bit."

"Really?" Ma asked, her voice full of the same shock I felt. I'd never heard those words from the doctor before and I'd never expected to. I'd been told very early on that my condition wouldn't improve and my medicines would just keep me from declining even further. So how had there been an improvement? I racked my brain to figure out if I'd started doing something new but the only thing I could remember was Raph's tea. Surely, some herbal tea couldn't be the reason I was better, right?

The doctor hummed as he closed my file. Dr. Merryweather was a quiet man. He was in his mid-fifties with short salt-pepper hair and kind blue eyes that always seemed just slightly pitying whenever he looked at me. But today, his eyes were lit with curiosity as he watched me and I wondered what he'd say if I told him the reason I felt better was herbal tea. He'd scoff at me, I was sure of that.

"You aren't taking any extra medicines, are you? You know how dangerous that can be, right?" He asked and I glared at him as I shook my head. He needed to stop before he made mom worry. Ma was a grizzly mama bear when it came to my health and if she even suspected that I was trying something stupid like self-medication, she'd drag me home and lock me in my old room.

"No, doctor. But I did start going on early morning walks. Maybe that has helped?"

He nodded, though he didn't look convinced. "Alright. Whatever it is, keep doing it. Maybe we'll see more improvement but don't put too much hope in it. It could just as well have been a fluke," he warned me, as if I didn't already know that. Most of my life had been a fluke, a *miracle* as Ma liked to call it and I knew there was a very real possibility I wouldn't live another five years. It was a fact that I'd accepted very early on in my life and it didn't phase me anymore. Much.

By the time we reached home, my head hurt and every muscle in my body felt like it'd been pulled through a wringer. I needed sleep. A lot of sleep and a lot of furry cuddles.

"Wait," Ma said as I grabbed the door handle. I turned towards her with a raised brow as Joy plopped a Tupperware box into my lap. "There. I made some food for you. I know you'll sleep for the next few hours, so stick this in the refrigerator and heat it when you're hungry, okay?"

I nodded as I grabbed the box and opened the door, "Joy, I'll see you on Saturday, okay? Bring an overnight bag."

Joy grinned at me and gave me a thumbs up. With a last I love you to both of them, I headed into my house.

Once I'd stuffed the Tupperware container in the refrigerator and changed into pajamas, I climbed into bed, feeling the exhaustion down to my bones. Padfoot clambered onto the bed before pressing up against me and plopping down on the bed, his light blue eyes watching me. I could almost imagine he was genuinely worried about me and I gave him a small smile and kissed his nose. "I'm okay, Pads. But I wouldn't mind some cuddle time." Padfoot licked my cheek in reply and I chuckled. I was so tired, but the pain in my head wouldn't let me sleep.

I grabbed my phone from where I'd dumped it on my nightstand and smiled when I saw a text from Raphael waiting for me.

Raph: Hey, let me know when you get home, okay?

The message had arrived half an hour ago, probably around the time I'd been in Dr. Merryweather's office. It explained why I hadn't seen it since I'd put my phone on silent.

Me: Hey, I'm home. Super tired. Was going to sleep but head hurts.

Raph: Can I come over? I'll just make you some tea and make sure you're okay. You don't even have to talk to me, I promise.

Me: You want to come over even though I'm tired and achy and won't do anything with you?

Raph: I know it's selfish but I just can't deal with the fact that you're hurting and alone and I'm so close and able to help and I'm not doing it.

Me: Are you kidding me? That's not selfish at all. If you really want to come, there's a key under a loose brick at the base of the stairs, on the right side. Tho, be warned: I can't promise I'd even get out of bed.

Raph: That's okay. See you in 5.

Was this man even real? Surely, no human could be that nice? I shook my head, immediately regretting it when the beat started pounding in my head again. I swear it felt like I could hear the blood pumping in my brain or something. Ugh, I hated the pain.

I closed my eyes, hoping Raph's tea would prove to be just as magical this time because I was *so* done with the pain.

Raphael

I knew I should have stayed away. I didn't want Jai to think that I was too needy or something. I had planned to only chat with him today. But how could I have stayed here all comfortable and relaxed when I knew my semnyar was just a few houses away, hurting? When I knew that I could help him, that I could make his pain less?

I hadn't been able to help myself from offering to come over. Now, here I was, grabbing the key from under the brick and inserting it into the keyhole.

Neya was off my shoulder and racing towards what I guessed was Jai's bedroom before I had the door closed behind me. This was the second time I was in his house, though I hadn't really looked around much last time because of the whole *he's my semnyar* revelation. I smiled at the huge, comfy looking couch that dominated the living room. There wasn't much else in the room other than a coffee table, the flat screen TV and a bunch of picture frames on the walls. I wanted to walk closer and check out all the photos but first I needed to make sure my semnyar was okay.

I couldn't stop thinking the word semnyar every time I thought about Jai. For most of my life, I'd assumed that just like my magic and my semlee, I wouldn't find my semnyar either. But here I was now, with all three of them. It was too good to be true, I knew that. And if the one hundred and fifty years of my life have taught me something, it was that good things always came to an end.

Even so, I was determined to make sure no harm came to Jai or Neya. I'd waited too long for them to let anything take them away from me now.

A picture of Jai lying in bed all cuddled up with Padfoot flashed in my mind and I realized I needed to get moving. All I wanted to do was go into the bedroom and hold Jai close to me, to let my magic sink into him and take away all his pain but I made myself go into the kitchen and put the kettle on. I needed to continue this ruse for a bit longer, at least until I could tell Jai without him immediately thinking I belonged in the loony bin.

His house had the same floor plan as mine, so working in his space wasn't too different. I'd brought the herbs with me and I poured a big mug of tea before making my way to the bedroom, careful not to wake Jai.

I smiled the moment I spotted him, the slight tightness in my chest melting away at the sight of me. He was dressed in pajama pants and an old t-shirt, his arms curled around the husky's huge torso as he slept. My smile widened when I realized Padfoot was awake and still not moving, just so his daddy wouldn't wake.

"You're such a good boy, Pads. Thank you for taking care of him," I told the doggo as I placed the mug on the bedside table before taking a seat at the edge of the bed. I pushed Jai's hair off his forehead, smiling when his nose scrunched up and he tried snuggling into my palm in his sleep like a cat. I made sure to keep my magic in check because I needed him to have some tea before I could heal him.

"Jai? I made some tea for you. I promise you'll feel better once you have it." Jai winced when I spoke, as if my voice hurt him, his eyelids fluttering for a moment before he opened them to squint at me.

"Raph?" He asked, his voice hoarse and sounding half-asleep.

"Yep, come on. I'll let you get right back to sleep once you drink the tea."

"Promise?" Jai asked, his voice softer.

"Promise," I agreed before helping him sit up. I handed him the mug and waited until he'd taken a few sips before pressing my palm against the back of his neck. I leaned forward, kissing his forehead and letting my lips linger as I closed my eyes and let the sight of my magic lead me.

I could see his body in a different light as I looked at him with my magic. Since the magic running through my veins was healing, I saw all the parts in his body that were hurting or damaged physically. I almost gasped aloud at how much pain he seemed to be dealing with. Is this what he felt every day or was today worse because of the hospital visit? I'd need to start keeping track of it.

I focused on the area that seemed to hurt the most—his head—and let my powers flow through him. I watched in relief as the red haze of pain around his head slowly started to disappear. I waited until it was almost gone before stopping. I wanted nothing more than to take away all of his pains, but I didn't have enough energy to do that. Plus, I also couldn't make him suspicious just yet. He had to believe it was the tea working here, not me.

I focused on some of the more painful parts of him, like his back and reduced the pain as much as I could. Once I had almost no magical energy left, I focused on his chest, wondering if I my magic would work on the permanent defects of his heart.

My own heart fluttered in my chest as I realized that my magic could do it. I didn't know how it was possible, since healing magic wasn't supposed to work on things like this, but my magic told me it could heal Jai. It would take a lot of time and dedication, a whole lot of energy too, but *I could do it*. I could heal my semnyar and make him whole again.

I pulled away as I realized just how long I'd been holding Jai like that and looked at him to realize he'd finished the tea. I took the mug from him, placing it on the table before taking his hands in mine, "Feel any better?"

He gave me a soft smile and nodded, his hair falling over his forehead as he did. I pushed the hair away so I could look into his eyes and smiled when I realized the haze of pain that had covered his eyes earlier was gone.

"Great. So I'll wash up and then head on home. You should get more sleep."

Jai nodded before biting his lip. He ran his fingers through Padfoot's fur as he spoke, not meeting my eyes, "Would you like to stay for a bit? Maybe we could watch something on Netflix?"

I was smiling before he'd finished talking. Did he feel it too? The bond that connected us? Did it make it difficult for him to stay away from me the way it did for me? I really, really hoped so.

"I'd love to," I answered honestly. If he'd just asked me to sit by his side while he slept, I would've still said yes.

SEVEN

Raphael

I straightened my shirt as I rang the doorbell. I couldn't believe how nervous I was considering the fact that I'd hung out with Jai more than once already.

This was different, though. This was a *date*. With my *semnyar*.

It had been so long since I'd been on an actual date—years maybe—and I had no clue if Jai would like what I'd planned for us tonight. Since I'd lived in Ravenshire for almost all my life, my only source of information regarding human date etiquettes were the books I'd read and the movies I'd watched. Maybe I should've left the planning to Jai. I had taken it upon myself because I'd wanted to impress Jai, but what if I ended up making a fool of myself? Jai would never give me a second chance if I messed up, right?

I was roughly pulled out of my thoughts as a big mass of fur collided with my middle, almost knocking me off the porch. I gasped as I grabbed the door-frame to steady myself as Padfoot rubbed himself all over me, leaving stray strands of fur on my clothes.

"Padfoot, stop it," Jai chided gently before looking up at me with an apologetic grin on his face. He was dressed in a dark blue hoodie with the words *Introvert Alert* in bold across the front and faded blue jeans. His glasses were slightly crooked and his hair was slicked back with gel, a single lock falling across his face. He looked like the perfect mix of sexy and sweet.

Jai looked down at himself as if to see what I was looking at before meeting my eyes and shrugging as he straightened his glasses. "I don't exactly go out much, much less on a date, so this was the best I could do."

His words made me feel just a bit less nervous since I wasn't the only one without experience here.

"You look perfect," I told him and his answering smile made my heart skip a beat in my chest. "And as far as dating goes, I haven't done much of that either, so if you don't enjoy what I've planned for us, will you give me a chance to take you on a do-over date?" I asked, my fingers slipping into my hair as I twirled a strand of my hair around my finger.

His eyes widened slightly at my confession before he gathered himself and smiled brightly at me. "I'm sure I'll enjoy whatever you've planned as long as I don't get too tired, but on the off-chance I don't, I promise to let you have a do-over. Now, come on in. Let me make sure Pads has enough food and water and then we can go." Jai called out Padfoot's name and the husky raced in from where he'd been nosing around the front yard.

"Come on, baby boy. Let's get you settled."

I followed the two and was just about to close the door when Neya raced in. I got the distinct impression she was angry with me because I'd left her playing in the backyard. She proved me right by racing after Padfoot without glancing my way. I shook my head at her dramatic ways as I closed the door.

"Oh I didn't see Neya with you," Jai's voice came from the kitchen and I headed there to see Neya proudly sitting on Padfoot's head.

"I think she followed me here," I admitted with a chuckle and a shot of annoyance rang through my new-ish bond with my semlee.

"Shall we?" I asked, waving towards the exit. Jai gave me a smile before leaning down and kissing the top of Padfoot and Neya's heads, making both of them puff up in pleasure.

A tinge of jealousy flashed through me—because I wanted a kiss too—and I knew Neya felt it because I could feel the smugness *rolling* off of her in waves. I rolled my eyes at her in my mind as I took Jai's hand and squeezed it gently before linking our fingers together. I planned on using our connection to send some of my magic into him if he started getting tired or hurting. For now, I brought up our linked hands and kissed the back of his.

This date was going to be perfect.

Jai

I grinned as Raphael talked a mile a minute, telling me about the job he'd scored at the animal shelter. He looked so happy to be helping the animals and his sweet excitement warmed my heart as we walked down the street.

We'd parked near the small park in the center of the town and I'd wondered for a moment if Raph intended on us taking a leisurely walk in the park. The weather seemed perfect for a walk to me, since the sun had almost disappeared behind a flock of clouds. I wasn't surprised since it was November and that meant the rain would be arriving soon. I loved rain, though I was glad it didn't look like it would rain today because I didn't want anything messing up our time.

Now as Raphael led me down a side street, I wondered exactly what he was planning because all I could see were tiny, cozy looking eateries. I'd love to check one of them out, but it was too early to think about dinner just yet. So where was Raph leading me?

My question was answered when Raphael stopped walking in front of a small doorway squeezed between two restaurants. I looked up at the handmade sign and a smile spread across my face as I realized what it was. *Betty's Books and Biscuits,* the old but well-preserved sign proclaimed.

"You brought me to a bookstore?" I asked, the glee clear in my voice as we stepped inside. A bell tinkled, signaling our welcome and I looked around the store with a smile. I'd never been here before, though I knew I'd be returning as soon as I spotted the comfy looking reading chair stashed in the corner of the room and the small counter that seemed to provide cookies and tea.

When I'd looked over the room once, noticing all the shelves and genres it catered to, my eyes drifted back to Raph, who was watching me as he twirled a lock of his hair around his finger, something I was quickly realizing was a nervous tic of his. I smiled at him so he knew I loved the place and an answering smile appeared on his face. "I thought maybe we could pick a favorite book for each other? And then I was thinking we could get takeout and go back to yours and read together for a bit? Or we could read here, if you prefer that."

My smile widened at his show of nerves because it just made him look even more adorable to me. After how confident he'd been every time we'd talked, I hadn't expected him to be so nervous, but I guess it told me this date meant just as much to him as it did to me, right?

"That sounds absolutely perfect," I said before pressing a kiss to the back of his hand and slowly untangling our fingers. "Let's pick a book then, shall we? Any genres you don't like? For me, it's classics and non-fiction."

Raphael smiled widely at me, shimmying in place as if he couldn't quite handle his excitement. "Same."

I chuckled at his adorableness before shaking my head and heading towards the fantasy section. I wanted to pick something magical for him, since his appearance into my life had been kind of magical too. Who could have thought I would find someone as sweet and lovely as Raph purely by chance?

What were the chances that the moment I'd started feeling like living was too much trouble he popped into my life and gave me a reason to try? What were the odds that he'd shown up to brighten up my half-life just when I'd given up on ever being normal?

I was still sick, and I'd be sick until I died, but with Raphael, all of it seemed like something that would happen years later, something that I didn't really need to think about right now.

I whooped silently when I spotted the perfect book for him and grabbed it off the shelf. *Throne of Glass* was the first in a seven book series, and I absolutely loved all of the books. I mean, who wouldn't adore a badass assassin like *Celaena*? I'd reread the series way too many times to count and I could've just lent Raph my own copies, but somehow buying a special copy just for him seemed even better.

I looked around the store and spotted Raphael still browsing a shelf, so I hurried over to the counter and got the book billed up. The sweet old lady behind the counter told me the cookies and tea were free and I could sit and read until the closing time if I wanted to. Why hadn't I known about this store before? How many more places like this existed in this small town that I didn't know about? How had I lived here for twenty-three years without knowing about this store?

"Could I have a pen, please?"

"Of course, my dear." The lady handed me a pen and I flipped open the book to the first page, smiling as I wrote a note for Raphael.

Because meeting you was like magic.

"Did you get a book?" Raph asked from behind me and I returned the pen before turning to face him, a smile on my face.

"Yep. What did you get me?"

He handed the book to the lady before I could see it, winking at me, his usual swagger back now that he was sure I was having fun. *So cute.*

Once he'd paid for his book, he held his hand out, palm up and we traded books. The one he'd bought for me was an indie book, and I realized with a smile that it was full of magic too.

"*The Enchanter's Flame*," I murmured as I read the blurb on the back. It sounded exactly the kind of book I enjoyed reading *and* it was a gay romance.

"Jai..." Raph murmured and I looked up to see him running his finger over the page. It took me a moment to realize he was reading the words I'd written in there and I smiled at him as I moved closer to him.

"It's true," I said with a smile and he flushed lightly before turning the book over to read the back of it.

"This sounds awesome! I can't wait to read it," Raphael exclaimed, a wide grin taking over his face.

"Me too. How about we get that takeaway and then go home and read? I'd love to read here sometime, but I think it'd be better if we get dinner first. I'm pretty sure we'd forget all about food if we started reading now."

"I'd never forget to feed you," Raph said with a serious look on his face, as if even the thought of me being hungry was abhorrent to him. Gods, was it weird that I wanted to pull his cheeks?

I smiled at him with a shake of my head before offering him my hand. It didn't take us long to find a cute little Mexican restaurant that offered some vegetarian options. We got some veg tacos and some bean and rice burritos before walking back to Raph's car.

We decided to head to mine since both our babies waited for us there. By the time we got home, my stomach was a growly mess from all the delicious aroma that filled the insides of the car.

"I'll dish up the food," I said as I headed into the kitchen with the takeaway bag, leaving Raph to deal with our excited fur-babies. I was surprised how not-tired I felt, considering we'd been out and about for almost two hours. I should've been exhausted by now, but instead I felt fresh as a daisy as I dished our food. What was that about? If I was being honest with myself, ever since I'd met Raphael, it seemed like I felt better and better each day. After all, hadn't my reports told me the same?

Could the fact that I was having fun, that I was actually, genuinely happy affect my health in some way? Because that had to be it, right? I was feeling better physically because I was in a better place mentally.

Whatever it was, I hoped it would never end because I was loving this new life I'd stumbled upon. I really, really hoped

Raphael wouldn't get sick of me, because I was already hooked on him.

We chatted all through dinner, talking about anything and everything. I realized that Raph had some issues with his family, though I couldn't figure out exactly what they were. I told him about my plans with my brother for the weekend and he seemed disappointed that we wouldn't get to have another date soon. Frankly, I was a bit disappointed about that too, but I was also looking forward to hanging out with Joy.

After I'd cleaned up the dishes with Raph's assistance, we settled down on opposite sides of the couch with our legs tangled in the middle, books in hand. Pads and Neya slept in Padfoot's bed and for the next few hours, we read in complete silence and it was the best first date ever.

When it was time for Raphael to leave, he did so reluctantly and I was just as hesitant to let him go.

"When will I see you again?" He asked as he walked backwards towards the door, his eyes never leaving mine.

"Monday? If you're free, that is."

Raphael smiled at me, changing course to walk closer until he was toe to toe with me. "I can't wait."

We stared into each other's eyes for a long moment, my eyes flickering to his full, pink lips that I wanted to taste so badly. I gathered up all my courage and asked, "Can I kiss you?"

Raphael's cheeks pinked as he nodded, and my palms framed his cheeks as I pulled him closer. The kiss was sweet, almost chaste as it began, our lips getting acquainted with the other's. His were so soft and so full that I couldn't stop myself from biting his lower lip lightly and tugging on it. He whimpered against me, a soft, breathy sound that shot straight to my groin. The kiss turned intense after that, our tongues reaching out, tangling, tasting. I cherished the sweet taste of him, never wanting to let ago.

Our bodies were pressed together, molded as one until there was no space between us. Pulling away from him seemed like the hardest thing in my life but I did it because I didn't want to rush this. Raphael was *good*, the best actually and I didn't want to rush anything with him. Plus, I hadn't done much of anything beyond kissing with anyone, so I was a little nervous about that too, though I was reluctant to tell that to Raph just yet.

He took a step back, his breathing as hard as mine, though he kept hold of my hand as if he couldn't bring himself to let go completely. "I guess I should get going."

He leaned forward and pressed his lips lightly to mine as Neya scrambled up his shoulder, somehow knowing it was time to leave. My eyes drifted close at the sweet touch of his lips and then he was gone, leaving behind his grassy scent and the taste of his lips on mine.

EIGHT

Jai

The doorbell rang just as I finished connecting the controllers. Perfect timing! I hopped to my feet, stumbling at the last second as my foot caught in the mess of wires and because I was a klutz. I grabbed the couch arm to keep myself from falling, cursing under my breath as I straightened up.

"Yo, *bhai*! Open up!" Joy's voice called from the other side of the door and I chuckled as I opened the door. Joy looked ready to start hammering the door, his fist lowering to his side as he grinned at me. He had a backpack slung over his shoulder, telling me he'd taken up my offer to stay the night. That was good. I missed hanging out with him, missed staying up late into the night playing games or watching anime with him.

"Come on in, *chhote*." I opened the door wide enough that he could get in without giving Padfoot a chance to make an escape. Neither me nor my brother had ever been to India, but Ma had made a point of teaching us a bit of her mother tongue—Hindi—when we were younger. I only knew the basics, but some words had stuck with us. We still called our mother, Ma and Joy preferred calling me Bhai. I called him chhote—the little one—once in a while, though I preferred calling him by his name since he wasn't especially fond of it. What kind of brother would I be if I didn't use his name to annoy him as much as I could?

"There's my prince!" Joy laughed loudly as Padfoot tackled him, and I grinned as they both tumbled on the floor. I couldn't play like that with Padfoot, and he never tried to, like he knew it'd hurt me. But watching the two of them tackle and roughhouse each other had me laughing in delight.

"All right kids, that's enough," I said, another chuckle escaping me as Padfoot licked a big stripe up Joy's cheek. Joy scrunched up his face and finally pulled away, sitting up and wiping his face with his shirt. His blond hair stood up in all directions and he ran his fingers through the strands in an unsuccessful attempt to straighten them.

"Video games?" He asked once he was standing and I nodded pointedly towards the couch where I'd set everything up. He grinned and rubbed his palms together. "Oh, I'm going to so kick your ass today, big bro."

I rolled my eyes at him in challenge, knowing I'd beat him like I always did. He may be the captain of his school's basketball team but I was the pro at video games and we both knew it.

Still, we spent the whole morning making stupid bets with me winning most of them. I had to let him win some, he was my little brother after all.

When it was time for lunch, Joy skipped into the kitchen, informing me dinner would be on me, just like it used to be when I lived with my parents. A sudden wave of homesickness washed over me as I thought about waking up to my parents making breakfast in the kitchen and Joy running around the house.

When I'd decided to leave, it hadn't been just because I wanted to be independent. It was also because I wanted to support myself at least a little bit. I earned enough as a content writer that I could afford to rent this place and feed myself and Padfoot, but not enough for my treatments and medicines. My parents still paid for that and though I wished I could do it myself, I knew I wasn't equipped for any kind of nine-to-five job to make that possible.

Ma hadn't been all that happy when I'd decided to move out, especially since she came from a culture where kids lived with their parents until they got married and sometimes even after that. She'd given in grudgingly at the end, extracting the promise from me that I'd come over for dinner every other week. She still kept my room exactly as it was, as if she expected me to give up on living alone and come back home sooner or later. Sometimes, I wanted to do just that.

My phone pinged on the coffee table and I smiled when I saw Raph's name on the screen.

Raphael: Hey handsome, what are you up to today?

Me: My brother's here for the weekend, remember? We spent all morning playing video games. You?

Raphael sent me a picture of a litter of kittens scrambling around what looked like him sitting cross-legged on the floor. I could only see his legs and part of his torso, encased in tight jeans that seemed to show off his fine thighs.

Raphael: Working at the animal shelter. Well, it's not really work if you enjoy it, right?

Me: True. Also, those kittens look adorable.

Raphael: Ikr? I'm calling them Cee, Dor and Coal.

Me: Hmmm...any particular reason for those names?

Raphael: Well, I just read this really awesome book my date gave me, so I named them after the characters.

Me: Aha! Celaena, Dorian and Chaol! Ha! Are you planning on reading the next book?

Another picture came in, this time with a book on his lap. It was the second book in the series.

Me: Damn. I still haven't finished the one you gave me :(

Raphael: You should spend time with your brother now. Read later. Though yeah, we can only meet after you've read it.

Me: WHAT? Why?

Raphael: *winks* Just because I can. I really want to know what you think about it.

Me: Okay. I'll blame you when I turn up at your door at four in the morning with huge dark circles under my eyes.

Raphael: Don't worry, I'll heal you right up.

Me: Heal me?

Raphael: My magic tea, remember?

Me: Oh yes, your magical herbal tea. How could I forget? You really are the healing angel, aren't you? xD

"Is that Cassian?" My brother asked and I looked up at him as he leaned against the kitchen doorway, arms crossed over his chest. How long had he been standing there without me noticing?

"Um, no," I mumbled, not meeting his eyes. I knew he'd noticed because he walked over to me before sitting on the couch beside me. I peeked at him and found him watching me with a raised brow. I flushed as I looked away again, chewing on my lower lip. It wasn't that Joy didn't know I was gay. Or that I didn't want to talk about Raph. I did. I wanted to gush about him. But I didn't date and Joy knew that.

"Um, well it's...my neighbor?" I don't know why the statement turned into a question as it passed my lips, but I knew he wouldn't believe me the moment it did.

"Bullshit," he shot back immediately and I winced. He was my closest friend, of course he knew I was lying. Well, technically I wasn't but I also wasn't telling him the truth.

"Well, um, he's...he's...I mean, we're dating," I said the words in a rush, hoping he wouldn't realize what I'd said. The wide grin on his face told me he'd heard exactly what I'd said.

"You sneak. We don't talk for a week and you have a boyfriend? What the fuck? Tell me everything!" You know how, in the books the siblings never want to hear about each other's dating lives? Well apparently, my brother hadn't gotten the memo.

I rolled my eyes at him before sinking into the couch and blowing out a breath as I tried to figure out what to tell him. " He's not my boyfriend. We just went on a date. His name is Raphael, he moved here a few weeks ago. I lost Pads while on a walk once and he helped me out. Anyway, we got to talking and I asked him out. We went on our first date yesterday."

"*You* asked *him* out?" Joy asked, staring at me with wide eyes.

"Well...we both asked each other out at the same time, " I confessed with a roll of my eyes. Could I sound any cheesier?

"Wow." He seemed to need a moment to gather his thoughts before he nodded at me. "Alright, invite him to lunch tomorrow."

"Why would I do that?" I asked with narrowed eyes. I knew his scheming face. I'd grown up seeing it right before he'd create some kind of mess for ma to clean up. This had disaster written all over it.

"What do you mean why? I gotta make sure this guy is good enough for you."

I shook my head at him but the look in his eyes told me that if I didn't do as he said, he'd go around knocking doors until he found Raph and he'd invite him himself.

I pulled out my phone with a sigh and tapped out a message to Raph.

Me: I know you said we can't hang out until I finish the book, but my brother wants to invite you for lunch tomorrow?

Raphael: Your brother wants to meet me?

The instant reply made me chuckle. I could almost feel his panic through the message.

Me: Yeah, my LITTLE brother is very insistent. Will you come?

Raphael: Of course. I'll be there.

Me: Perfect. Pro tip: Ignore everything he tells you about me.

"Hey! I was only gonna tell him the good things," Joy spoke up, telling me he'd read everything.

I rolled my eyes at him before looking around the empty room. "How about you focus on today's lunch for now?"

He poked his tongue out at me before heading back to the kitchen and I gave myself a moment to think about everything. Joy would meet Raphael tomorrow. Damn.

Raphael

I watched as the new cat mom cleaned her kittens. I'd helped that happen. I'd used my magic to make sure the cat didn't die. The vet at the shelter had told me the mama cat had cancer and they believed she wouldn't survive the birth since she was so weak. But here she was, feeding her tiny little babies. All because of me. I couldn't help feeling proud of myself. So what if my magic couldn't heal gunshot wounds or a burn victim?

I'd saved three kittens from ending up orphaned and I'd be proud of it if it was all I got to do with my magic.

It wasn't though, because my magic could help Jai too. I still didn't know if my magic worked on him because of our bond or because my magic was just different. What if it *was* different? What if, instead of being the weakling I was the only healer who could heal born illnesses and cancer? If that was true, what would my parents say when I told them?

They'd be proud of me, I realized and though it was all I'd ever wanted, somehow the thought tasted bitter. Why should I be happy at their appreciation now when they'd spent all their time secretly wishing I wasn't their son? Even if they had never been outright hostile towards me, there had been enough barbed comments and whispered admonishments to tell me exactly what they thought of me. Yeah, no way was I telling them about this, even if it did turn out that my powers were unlike anyone else's and not *less*.

"Wow, she's alive?" A voice piped up behind me and I turned to smile at Rebba, the woman who managed the shelter. She was a big woman, just an inch or so shorter than my 6'2" frame with black dreadlocks framing her face. She had a wonder-filled smile on her lips as she walked closer and knelt beside me, joining me as I watched the cat family.

"They're adorable," she breathed out in a whisper before shooting me a smile. "You have natural talent with these animals, don't you? You got a pet?"

I gave her a sheepish grin as I scratched the back of my neck. Did a semlee count as a pet? "Um, I have a squirrel."

She blinked at me, her mouth falling open just a tad bit. Oh. Did humans not have pet squirrels? But pet lizards were okay? And if that was so, why hadn't Jai said anything?

"You have a pet...squirrel?"

"Well, she lived in my backyard, but she got hurt. So I patched her up and then she decided to move in with me," I answered with a shrug and Rebba gave a loud, booming laugh that had the mother cat hissing at us as her kids mewled softly.

"Oh, sorry baby. I'll keep it low," Rebba cooed immediately, her voice softening as she went back to watching the cats.

"What do you think about adopting one of these when they grow up a bit?" Rebba offered and I turned to watch the three kittens I'd christened Cee, Dor and Coal. Coal, as per his name, was coal black. Since he wouldn't open his eyes for a few days yet, he was all black for now. Cee was a cute, gray cat with darker gray patched decorating her back while Dor was orange and white. They were all adorable and if I could have it my way, I'd adopt all of them. Well, technically nothing was stopping me from adopting all of them. I had enough money and room. I'd have to discuss it with my roommate though. Neya wouldn't like it if I sprung a surprise like this on her.

"I'll think about it," I told Rebba and she nodded at me before getting to her feet. I followed suit since I couldn't exactly spend the whole day staring at those adorable kittens. I stopped short at the curious look Rebba was giving me and raised my brow at her in question.

"I've wondered for a while, but it's making more and more sense...are you a supe, Raphael?" Rebba asked and my eyes widened involuntarily.

"Um..." I mumbled helpfully as Rebba continued.

"I thought I scented it when you first came here, but the scent of your magic was very faint in the beginning. It's thicker now, more noticeable."

If she could scent my magic, it meant she was a supe—supernatural—too. I narrowed my eyes at her as I tried to figure out what she could be. "Shifter?"

Rebba grinned at me and slapped my back, making me almost fall over. "Yep, you're a mage, I'm guessing?"

I nodded, feeling relieved that she knew. Now I wouldn't have to hide what I did for these animals from Rebba.

"Good. So you can heal animals, huh? That's great. I'm glad you could help Mama Cat over there."

I smiled and shrugged my shoulders, hoping she wouldn't ask questions. I really didn't want to tell her why I was working here or about my past.

"Alright, I'm heading back out. Poor Coop is very anxious and I want to spend some time with him."

I nodded as she left the room and let out a relived sigh. My thoughts drifted towards Coop. He was an old pug who had been abandoned by his supposed family when he started going blind. Apparently, they'd only liked him when he was cheerful and active. Assholes. I wanted to try and help Coop. If I couldn't take away his blindness, at the very least I'd try to take away the pain and anxiety he must be feeling.

Like they did every time since I'd met Jai, my thoughts went back to him the moment my head was clear. I'd be meeting his brother tomorrow. Shit. If this were anyone else, I'd feel like things were going too fast. The only reason it didn't feel rushed was because I could feel the bond we shared. He was my semnyar, the one fate had chosen for me. It didn't matter if we rushed or took it at tortoise pace, we'd still end up together. I couldn't have picked a better person for myself. Jai needed taking care of and I was a caretaker down to my core. At the same time, Jai had this underlying assuredness, a confidence that drew me towards him. He was shy sometimes, but never overtly so and his quiet strength drew me in. He might seem weak to some people with his tiny size and all the medicines he needed, but the moment I'd seen him through the sight of my magic, I'd known that as nothing but a lie. The amount of pain he lived with *daily* told me he was much stronger than anyone gave him credit for. I couldn't even imagine living like that for a single day, much less my whole life.

I didn't know where things would go with us, but I knew two things for sure: a) I'd never, ever give up on Jai and our bond and b) I'd give him every drop of magic I had if it would heal him, and I wouldn't stop until he had the life he deserved to live.

NINE

Raphael

Why was I so nervous? I was one hundred and fifty years old, for mother's sake! I'd faced off worse people than a seventeen year old kid and yet here I was, pacing around my living room with not a clue how to handle this lunch. Would I seem good enough for Jai in his brother's eyes? What if he didn't like me? Would that mean Jai wouldn't go out with me anymore?

I shook my head to get rid of the reckless thoughts and glanced at the clock, realizing it was time. Shit. I raced back to my room and ran a comb through my hair since I'd managed to mess it up in my anxiety. Again.

It was only after I'd locked my front door and taken a few steps—with Neya on my shoulder because she could feel my panic and wanted to comfort me—that I realized I didn't even know Jai's brother's name. Crap. Why hadn't I asked him that before?

Cursing myself, I walked the three blocks to Jai's house, my heart thudding erratically in my chest as I wiped my sweaty palms on my jeans. I wasn't usually this nervous, not about *anything*. But this was my semnyar and his brother, and I wanted him to like me. Jai and I were meant to be together, but I wanted his family to like me too. In my imagination, Jai's family would accept me and love me like they loved Jai, like my own parents never had. They'd call me their son and hug me and tell me they were proud of me, things I'd always yearned for from my own parents but had never gotten.

The fanciful thoughts helped calm down a little and by the time I was knocking on Jai's front door, I felt almost back to normal. The door was opened by a teen with blond hair and blue eyes and it took me a long minute to reconcile the fact that this was Jai's brother. It clicked when the boy smiled, because that smile was exactly like Jai's.

"Hey, you must be Raphael, come on in," he said, stepping back to let me in as Pads scrambled over to greet me. Jai's brother closed the door behind me as I leaned forward to pet Padfoot, taking a few moments extra to make sure I wouldn't blurt something stupid in my attempt to make him like me. Taking the chance, Neya scrambled off my arm and onto Padfoot's back, a feeling of calm reassurance washing over me through our bond as she left.

"Is that a squirrel?" Jai's brother asked, surprise coloring his voice.

I turned back to look at him, still having a hard time believing that this guy who looked like the captain of a football team was my semnyar's brother. He was bulky, with muscles straining against his t-shirt and almost as tall as me. Except for that smile, he looked nothing like his brother.

Before I could answer him, I felt Jai's presence in the room and turned around with a smile. Even though we'd spent hours together the day before yesterday, I felt like I hadn't seen him in years. He stood in the kitchen doorway, an apron wrapped around him, his glasses slightly foggy from steam as he squinted through them. I quietly sent a wisp of my magic—not my healing magic, but the inherent, shapeless magic that all mages possessed and could mold into whatever they needed it to be—washing over the glasses and clearing them up. Jai smiled, though he looked confused and I did a mental face-palm because I needed to tell him about my magic soon.

"Hey Raph, this is my brother, Joy. Joy, this is Raphael," he introduced us and my eyes widened at their names as I grinned.

"Really?" I asked, looking between the two of them. I knew some parents gave similar names to their kids, but I'd only seen that happen when the kids were twins. Jai and his brother looked as different from each other as they could have while still sharing their DNA.

Jai rolled his eyes at my amusement as he walked closer. Without missing a beat, I leaned forward and kissed his cheek, only stopping myself from kissing his lips because of his brother. Even so, Joy didn't miss the chance to go "Awww" behind us and Jai rolled his eyes again, even though I could see he was trying not to smile.

"My mom named me and when Joy was born she told my dad to do the honors. Apparently, my dad couldn't think of anything else."

"I think he put a lot of thought in it, actually," I said as we walked towards the kitchen, Joy following close on my heels.

"And how did you figure that?" Joy asked from behind me and I shot him a grin as I answered.

"Well, the two of you look nothing alike, right? If I hadn't known, I never would've guessed you're brothers. But when you say, this is Jai and this is Joy, it's kinda obvious that you're related, right? At the very least, it would make people wonder."

"Hmm...I guess dad hadn't been as careless as I thought after all," Joy mused and I wondered what he meant by that.

As we ate lunch, I stayed silent for the most part, enjoying watching Jai interact with his brother. He was so free like this, slugging his brother, laughing out loud. If I hadn't known, if I hadn't seen it with my own magic, I'd never believe he was in pain right now. But I had and he was. I couldn't touch him right now, I wasn't sure if he'd be okay with that in front of his brother, but I wanted to just so I could take some of that pain away.

My eyes drifted to Joy and I wondered what his life was like. He was around six years younger than Jai and I couldn't imagine what his life had been like. I was glad to see that Joy didn't hold any resentment towards his brother.

Working at the hospital with my parents, back when they'd still hoped I'd get my powers, I'd watched so many siblings dislike their brother or sister for getting sick and messing up their plans, as if they had intentionally done that. I was glad Jai's brother didn't seem to think in that vein because I really wanted to like him and not hurt him. He seemed like a nice enough guy and it was clear Jai loved him.

Watching the two of them had me missing Sera. I hadn't seen my little sister since I moved here and I wondered if she'd ever come over to see me or would she follow our parents' order to stay away from me? Before I'd left Ravenshire, my parents had warned me that if I left, I'd never be allowed to come back. After all, they were better off without a mage with broken magic. They were important, the best healers in the world. They didn't need someone like me ruining their reputation.

I'd hoped my sister would stay in contact, since we'd always been close and she'd always defended me against the others even though she was twenty years younger than me. But she hadn't. She hadn't once sent a message or even her semlee to check on me. Nothing. She'd abandoned me, just like everyone else.

Jai

Joy left once lunch was done since he was meeting some friends later, but not before dragging me into the bedroom with the excuse that he needed some advice from me. Yeah, right.

As soon as we were in the room, he pulled me into a hug, squeezing the life out of me with those muscles of his before pulling back and grinning at me. "How the fuck did you manage to hook that hottie, *bhai*?"

I swatted at his arm, not that it would hurt him at all. "Shut up."

"But seriously, he seems like a nice guy. I mean, he rescued a squirrel and works at an animal shelter. Seems like he was made just for you."

I chuckled at the dig at my animal love even though I agreed with him. Raph was everything I hadn't known I needed and even though I didn't know him all that well just yet, I knew he was a good man.

"I like him, Jai. He's good to you. But if he ever does anything to hurt you, you let me know, okay? I will kick his ass." The tone of his voice told me exactly how serious he was and my heart warmed at how much he cared for me. I was so lucky to have him for a brother.

"I will, *chhote*. I love you."

"I love you too, *bhai*. Now, I gotta go."

Once he was gone, I looked for a reason to make Raphael stay. He'd seemed lost in thought while we ate and I could almost feel his sadness. I'd no clue what he'd been thinking of and I didn't think I had the right to pry. I didn't want him going back home, though. Not yet.

"Hey, I'm just about done with the book. Why don't you stay for a bit and maybe we could read together? I have a copy of the book you were reading," I said, referring to the book he'd sent me the picture of.

Raph smiled at me, his face lighting up and telling me he was just as happy with the prospect of staying.

"Great. I'll get the books." I made my way to my bedroom and the bookshelf that spanned the length of one whole wall, walking over to the fantasy section and picking out *Crown of Midnight* for Raphael.

I grabbed my copy of *The Enchanter's Flame* off the bedside table, a bolt of pain shooting over my spine as I leaned forward. Shit. I'd managed to ignore the pain for the most part during lunch, but sitting straight for so long had wrecked my back. I hoped Raph wouldn't mind lounging on the couch while we read.

In the living room, I found Raph seated on the couch, playing with Padfoot's ears while he lay on the floor at his feet.

"Here you go." I handed him the book as I sat beside him, wincing as another shot of pain traveled up my spine.

"Scoot over," Raph said as he pulled his legs up on the couch and we splayed over the couch, heads on opposite ends like last time. My back thanked me profusely as I lay down and a sigh escaped my lips.

"You okay?" Raph asked, a frown on his face. Putting the book away, he grabbed my feet and pulled them towards him, massaging the arch of my foot. I couldn't stop myself from moaning at how exquisitely good it felt. His touch warmed my skin in a way nothing else did, and I relaxed into the couch as he kept up the pressure, his palms rubbing up my calf every once in a while.

After what felt like hours but was probably only a few minutes, Raph pulled away and I opened my eyes just the tiniest bit—I hadn't even realized I'd closed them—to see him smiling at me. "Better?"

It was, I realized with surprise. The pain in my back had all but disappeared and so had the exhaustion I'd been feeling after cooking the meal. All I felt at that moment was warm and sleepy. How?

"Your touch is like magic," I mumbled sleepily and Raph's smile widened as he trailed his fingers up my leg. If I wasn't feeling so delightfully warm and comfy, his touch would've turned me on, but I was too sleepy at the moment for my body to react.

"Do you believe in magic?" Raphael asked, and I was surprised at how serious he looked. It wasn't just curiosity making him ask. There was something else in his eyes, but I was too sleepy to try to figure out what it was.

"That's the second time someone has asked me that question in the last few days," I told him, chuckling at the strangeness of it.

"It is?"

I nodded. "Cassian, he's my best friend. He asked me the same question a few days ago. I'll tell you what I told him."

Raphael leaned forward, his green-brown eyes focused on me as he waited for me to speak. "I'm a believer. I like books with witches and magical creatures." I shook the book still in my hand in emphasis. "If someone told me magic was real and proved it to me in some way, then I'd definitely believe them because I can't believe that magic *doesn't* exist. Too many things happen in this world that seem impossible to believe magic doesn't exist..."

I trailed off at the wide smile on Raphael's face and waited for him to say something. Was he about to laugh at my reasoning?

"I believe the same," he told me, his voice barely above a whisper as he leaned forward to caress my cheek with his palm. I sank into his touch and that same warmth drew me in, making me feel sleepy and comfier than I ever was.

I heard Raphael say something, but I'd already started to drift off and the words floated away as I fell asleep, feeling safe and cared for with my angel near me.

TEN

Jai

I looked out the window at the downpour. I've always loved watching the rain, but when I watched it now, it didn't fill me with the same sense of joy it usually did. Something was missing.

It took me a few moments to realize what my heart wanted, but once I did, I was out of the door before I could tell myself I was being stupid.

I was not an impulsive guy. My health had never allowed me to be. Yet, I found myself running down the three blocks that separated my house from Raphael's, laughing as the rain drenched through my flimsy clothes. We'd spent almost the whole of yesterday together and yet my heart wanted more. I wasn't sure if the things I felt for Raph were supposed to happen so...quickly. It had barely been around two weeks since I met him and already, I couldn't bring myself to think about a life without him. Raphael had grown on me and I didn't think I'd ever want him to leave. There was something pulling me to him. Something that made it impossible for me to stay away from him. But did Raph feel the same? Or was I the only one who felt this tug pulling me to him?

I was shivering as I reached Raphael's place, but it didn't stop me from hammering my fist at his door in my eagerness.

"What the..." Raphael started as he took in my rain soaked appearance but I grabbed his hand and pulled him out of the doorway with me before he could continue.

I pulled him under the open sky with me, grinning at him as the rain showered over the both of us, soaking his clothes until he was as wet as me, his blond hair darkening to a soft brown as it became wet.

"Jai? Why are we standing in the rain?"

"Because I really, really wanted to do this," I said as I leaned up and pressed my lips to his. His lips were soft and warmer than mine and I sighed as their gentle warmth surrounded my lips.

My arms curled around his waist, holding him to me tightly as my tongue traced his lower lip, tasting the sweet rain water on them. Raph moaned low in his throat, his arms slipping around me, his palms firm on my ass as he pulled me closer.

I don't know how long we kissed under the rain, how long we stood there, so close there was barely any space between us. We kissed like we had all the time in the world, and maybe, just maybe, we did. A guy could wish, right?

The rain stopped before we did, but once it did, my body caught up with how thoroughly drenched I was. A shiver wrecked through me, making Raph pull away from me, his eyes full of concern as he looked me over.

"Come on, let's get you inside before you catch a cold. That was the best kiss of my life and I don't want it to end with my boyfriend getting sick, okay?"

I was silent as he grabbed my hand and led me towards his house, not just because I knew my teeth would start chattering if I opened my mouth but also because I couldn't stop thinking about what he'd said.

The best kiss of his life. With me.

As if that in itself wasn't enough, he'd called me his boyfriend. Fuck.

My heart bubbled with joy as I followed my boyfriend inside, knowing he'd take care of me like he always did. He was my healing angel, after all.

Raphael

I shook my head at Jai's strange impulsiveness even as my lips tingled at the memory of that kiss. I hadn't been lying when I told him it was the best kiss of my life. I'd never wanted to stop, but when Jai had started shivering from the cold, I'd known it was time to get inside. I'd also called him my boyfriend even though we hadn't discussed it yet. The thing was, Jai was it for me. Maybe he wasn't there yet but for me, he was everything. Boyfriend seemed like such a simple and unworthy word for what he was to me, but it was the best I could do until I tell him everything.

Water dripped from my hair and clothes as I led Jai into the bathroom, but I ignored my own wetness as I grabbed a fluffy towel off the rack before turning to my sweet man, who looked like he was clenching his teeth to keep them from chattering. His arms were crossed across his chest tightly and I could swear his fingers had turned blue from the cold. Did his illness affect his body's ability to warm up too?

Pulling him closer, I plopped the towel on his head before rubbing it around until his hair was as dry as I could manage without a dryer. I hadn't really needed to dry his hair since I was about to ask him to get a shower anyway, but I'd still done it for some reason that I couldn't put my finger on. Maybe I just wanted a reason to hold him.

"Wait here," I told him as I walked back into my room, making a note to wipe all the water off the floors as soon as I'd changed. Riffling through my closet, I pulled out a thick, comfy hoodie and pajama pants that I hoped wouldn't be too big on him. I also grabbed a pair of underwear, since I knew his clothes were soaked all the way in. After all, so were mine and he'd been outside longer than I had.

"Here you go," I told him as I handed him the clothes. "I think you'd feel better after a hot shower."

Jai nodded in jerking motions as he grabbed the clothes from my hand. I nodded towards the kitchen as I spoke, "I'll get changed and make some tea while you're in, okay?"

Jai took a deep breath and the words rushed out before he clamped his mouth shut again to keep his teeth from chattering. "You aren't cold?"

"Magic." I winked at him as he smiled at the word, shaking his head before shuffling into the bathroom and closing the door behind him. I wanted nothing more than to get in there with him and help him warm up, but I wasn't sure we were there yet.

I busied myself changing into a similar outfit before throwing my wet clothes in the laundry. I made a note to wash them tonight so I wouldn't end up with a room that smelled like wet laundry before making my way to the kitchen.

Instead of the tea I'd promised Jai, I found myself making one of the herbal drinks my mom used to make for the colder days. Our magic prevented us from getting sick, but we still felt cold when the weather made us. My mom's herbal drink had always been my favorite because it wasn't just healthy but also tasted pretty damned good. You could say it was our version of hot chocolate. Just healthier and without the chocolate.

I grabbed the kettle and put some water on before adding all the herbs I remembered my mom using. The basil and ginger were what made it taste so good, while the black pepper and the other herbs and spices added to its health benefits.

I put the brew to simmer as I walked to the hall closet and grabbed my favorite blanket before placing it on the couch for Jai. It was a woven wool blanket that I'd made myself a few years ago, and it remained my favorite because I'd used the softest yarn I could find. It was the perfect blanket to cuddle in and I was hoping to do some of that before Jai went home.

The sound of footsteps had me putting away the strainer I'd been using and I smiled at the sight of Jai in my clothes. The hoodie was slightly bigger on him, with only his fingers peeking out of the sleeves. He'd folded the pant cuffs a few times to make them fit and he looked absolutely adorable in my clothes, especially with the glasses that had somehow managed to slip to the tip of his nose yet again.

"Why don't you take a seat on the couch? I'll bring the drinks over and then we can maybe watch a movie?" I asked and I could clearly hear the hope in my voice. I knew he probably wanted to get back to Padfoot soon—I'd discovered very soon that he didn't like leaving his baby alone for too long—but I also hoped he'd want to spend time with me. We hadn't planned this, and I had to get to the shelter in a few hours for my shift, but I wanted to spend time with him before I had to leave.

"That sounds p-perfect," Jai said and though there was a slight stutter in his voice that told me he was still cold, he looked much better than he had before. His fingers were back to their normal color and he wasn't holding himself stiffly either.

I followed him into the living room, a tray with two big mugs of the drink in my hands and smiled as he picked up the blanket, rubbing it against his face with a soft smile playing on his lips, his eyes fluttering close as if he wanted to only focus on his sense of touch for a moment.

As I took the seat beside him and placed the tray on the coffee table, he turned to me, the smile firmly in place. "Where did you get this blanket? It's so soft."

I smiled at his open appreciation, feeling proud that he liked something I'd made. "I made it."

His eyes went wide behind his square glasses, his lips forming an o of surprise and I found myself blushing for no reason other than he was looking at me with something akin to wonder. It was a look I'd hoped to see on him when I told him about my magic, but seeing it in reply to something so much simpler somehow made it feel even better. I really hoped he'd react the same way when it came to my magic. I didn't want to hide it from him, not if our relationship was to have any kind of future. I'd read enough paranormal romances to know that hiding things like that for too long was never a good idea.

As we cuddled under the couch and watched the movie, I mulled over how I'd tell him about my magic. I remembered what he'd said yesterday about believing in magic, that if he saw proof of it, he'd definitely believe in it.

Now, how to prove it to him?

"Hey Raph?" Jai asked a few minutes later, his voice soft. I paused the movie so I could focus on him, though he seemed determined to look anywhere but at me.

"Yeah?"

"You called me your boyfriend before..." He trailed off, and I wasn't sure if he'd liked that or not. Did I apologize or did I tell him how I felt?

"I did. I'm sorry, we should've talked about it, right?"

"Did you mean it? Do you want to be my boyfriend? Despite all my issues?"

I tipped his chin upwards so he was looking at me, his brown eyes wary and hopeful as they met mine. "I meant every word, Jai. I told you before, your issues as you called them, don't bother me. I like taking care of you and I like *you*. I'd love to be your boyfriend."

Jai smiled and leaned up, pressing a soft kiss on the underside of my chin before snuggling closer. He turned towards the TV again and I took the hint and hit play, a wide smile on my own face. Jai could feel the bond too, whether he knew what it was or not.

My phone buzzed from somewhere on the couch, reminding me I needed to get ready to go to the animal shelter soon. And there my answer to my earlier question was, staring back at me from the screen of my phone.

"Hey Jai, would you like to come to the animal shelter with me?"

ELEVEN

Raphael

The rain had stopped by the time I needed to leave for my shift at the shelter, so Jai left to change into dry clothes and make sure Pads had everything he'd need. I took the time to change into my work clothes, glad that I worked at a place that required me to wear old t-shirts and faded jeans because that pretty much summed up my wardrobe. Most of the clothes I'd had back in Ravenshire would look tacky here. We didn't wear cloaks and robes like the wizards from Harry Potter, but the leather belts and bright clothes weren't something I could wear here without coming off as a hippie or a weirdo. I'd left most of my clothes at the house, only taking the few *common people* outfits I owned. I'd shopped for some more clothes after I met Jai—I wanted to impress him, of course—but I reserved those clothes for when we went out.

I tied off my hair at the base of my skull, something I only did for work because I didn't want it to get dirty and grabbed my phone before heading outside. I'd checked over Coop—the blind dog who'd been abandoned by his family—with my magic and I knew I could heal him. I'd been shoring up my magic so I could do it in one go, and what better way to show Jai my powers than to heal an animal in front of him? Other than healing Jai, that was my favorite thing about my newfound power. I knew I could levitate a few leaves or do something equally easy to show Jai my magic, but I wanted to show it to him in a way that wasn't so...frivolous.

Jai looked a bit out of breath when he reached my car, so I pulled him into a quick kiss, sending some of my magic into him to calm his lungs. He pulled away after a minute, giving me a soft smile before jumping on his toes.

"Oh, I'm so excited! I love animals. I'd always wanted to adopt an animal from a shelter or maybe foster home, but I couldn't with all my shit. Maybe I could just volunteer where you work? Do they allow that?"

"Of course," I answered with a grin as I opened the passenger door of my car for him. He shot me a grin before getting seated and I walked around the front and got into the driver's side.

I told him about all the animals at the shelter as I drove, or at the very least, the ones I was friends with. We arrived at the shelter while I was telling him about Rebba. She appeared a bit intimidating at first glance and I wanted to make sure Jai knew she wasn't.

"Hey Raphael, you brought a friend?" Rebba called out from the back of the main room where she seemed to be sorting through crates of dog food.

"Rebba, this is my boyfriend, Jai. Jai, my lovely boss, Rebba."

Jai smiled at Rebba and waved at her while she looked him over before shooting me a grin. "You did good, man." Turning to Jai, she smiled warmly at him. "Hey Jai, are you wanting to adopt one of the babies or just visiting?"

"Visiting, I think. But after being surrounded by a bunch of fluffies, who knows?" Jai said, shrugging his shoulders. I laughed at his declaration before pulling him into my arms.

"Come on, I want you to meet Coop. Hey Rebba, let me know if you need help hauling those into the storage, okay?"

Rebba mock-glared at me, flexing her arms in a move that I translated to *I got all the muscles I need* and I raised my hands up in surrender before leading Jai into the next room, the dog room as we called it.

I led him towards the kennel that housed Coop, being intentionally soft-footed since Coop was asleep. "This is Coop. His family abandoned him because he's old and blind."

Jai tensed in my arms before cursing Coop's family under his breath. "Assholes. He's so adorable. How could they kick him out?"

Coop was adorable. He was a pug and he was all saggy skin and a lolling tongue, a white film over his dark eyes and stubby legs that he tottered about on when he was feeling well.

I pulled Jai closer to me, turning his face so he was looking into my eyes. I took a deep breath. This was it. Time to see if Jai had really meant what he'd said. "Jai, Coop is blind and very weak from old age. You can ask Rebba to confirm it or see his vet reports." I chewed on my lower lip as I wondered how to continue and Jai's brows furrowed, obviously confused as to why I was telling him that.

Steeling myself, I continued speaking, hoping he'd believe me. "Yesterday, you told me you would believe in magic if you were shown proof of it. So I hope you'll believe me when I tell you that...that I'm a mage and I have powers, magic if you will."

Jai's eyes widened steadily as I spoke, but not in disbelief. There was surprise but there were other emotions there too, emotions that said that maybe he would believe me. Awe and...hope.

Jai

When Raphael had asked me if I believed in magic, I had not expected him to tell me it was real. I'd always hoped it was, of course, ever since I was a little kid. I'd always had more imaginary and fictional friends than real ones, and I'd always hoped they were real, that the magical world they lived in was real. It had been a little kid's hope, I admit, but I'd never been able to let go of it. I'd always hoped that there was something beyond the ordinary in this world. It had been a selfish hope, to be honest. I'd hoped for some kind of magic that would make me...normal. Healthy. Save me from having to live a short and pain filled life. And now Raphael was telling me that magic was real...

I didn't know what to think, but I'd told Raph I would believe it if someone proved it to me and I had meant that. After all, that's how science worked, so why not magic? I smiled at him hesitantly and whispered, "Show me?"

The smile on Raphael's face was blinding as he nodded and kissed my cheek before pulling away. Kneeling in front of the cage, he opened the door as I watched with rapt attention. What was he going to do? Coop woke up from his nap at the sound and sniffed his way closer to Raph, apparently recognizing his scent. It was clear he was blind from the way he moved with his head cocked to the side so his ear was facing us and his gait told me he was in pain. What was Raphael going to do to him? I knew he wouldn't hurt the dog, so maybe he could make him better somehow?

I knelt beside him so I could watch closely as he scratched Coop's chin before placing his palm flat on the dog's back. "Watch."

I watched his hand for a few moments but nothing happened, so I turned my gaze towards him and swallowed a gasp as my eyes widened. Raph's green-brown eyes were glimmering with a green light, a soothing green that seemed to make his eyes shine bright.

I turned my head to stare at Coop again and this time, I did gasp because the white film over Coop's eyes had disappeared and he was looking up at Raphael and I knew he was actually seeing him. Raphael had given Coop his sight back.

After a few moments, Raphael pulled away with a pained gasp and Coop jumped up on him, looking and acting years younger than he was and I watched in awe as he licked Raph's face in thanks, seemingly understanding who had made him better, before scrambling over to me. I petted him for a few moments, laughing at his utter delight, before turning to Raph.

He was sitting on the ground, arms around his knees as he watched me warily, waiting for my reaction. Even if I hadn't believed him, I wouldn't have been able to stop myself from giving him a smile just to get that fear out of his eyes. I'd seen what he did though, with my own two eyes. I'd seen the magic and it was real. I knew it would take me some time to process it all, but I believed him. He had magic and he had the ability to heal animals with it.

"You really are my healing angel, aren't you?" I said, my voice soft as I opened my arms for a hug.

Relief washed over his face and he scrambled closer before pulling me into an awkward hug with me sitting and him kneeling in front of me. "You believe me?"

"Of course, I believe you. You know you'll have to tell me everything now, right? I'm so curious about so many things."

"I will," Raphael said with a laugh before pulling away, his voice sounding slightly hoarse. "Can I come over after my shift? You can take my car and I'll get a cab or something."

"I can take a cab, don't worry."

"It's cool. I prefer not driving anyway. I didn't really need a car where I lived before."

"Don't make me even more curious when I have to leave!" I exclaimed, my voice thick with exasperation which only made him laugh. I rolled my eyes as I stood up, my spine cracking painfully as I straightened up.

Raph followed suit, pulling me into his arms and kissing me softly. Like every time he touched me, the pain that was always humming in the background muted. But unlike every other time, I knew something now that I hadn't before.

I pulled away from him, still holding his hands as I spoke, "Do you use your magic on me?"

Raphael flushed and shuffled on his feet, answering my question without speaking a word. As I thought back over all the times he'd made the pain disappear, the thought struck me. "It was never the tea or the massages, was it? It was your magic that took the pain away."

He nodded, looking wary though I wasn't sure why. I jumped on him, hugging him hard and letting him know just how much that meant to me. "Thank you," I whispered against his collarbone.

"I don't want you suffering," he said with a shrug, holding onto me just as tightly, "and if there's something I can do to take your pain away, then I'm going to do it."

I pulled away so I could kiss him again, tasting the sincerity of his words on his lips. Backing away was a struggle, but I knew he needed to get back to work. And I should probably go home and process everything he'd revealed. Even though it didn't change the way I felt about him, it still was a lot to take in. Magic was real. My boyfriend was a mage. Ugh, please don't let this be a dream. I didn't want to wake up and realize I'd been dreaming all of this.

"See you this evening? I'll make dinner."

"You're spoiling me with all the home-cooked food," Raphael complained, though he was smiling widely as he did, the relief that I'd believed him still clear in his eyes. Of course I believed him, I'd seen what he could do with my own eyes. More than that, I'd experienced it first hand, albeit unknowingly. Raphael was my angel and I knew I'd be holding onto him for as long as I was allowed to.

TWELVE

Jai

I stirred the stew as I thought over everything Raph told me. He was a mage. He could do magic. Goddamn. I wondered if I was dreaming and if I was, could I never wake up, please?

I knew I might have accepted the whole thing pretty easily. But honestly, I had no reason to doubt Raphael, did I? What would he get from lying to me about something like this? I'd felt what he could do, even if I hadn't known what it was at the time. All those times I'd credited his tea for making me feel better, it had been him. It had been his magic that had taken the pain away. And what did that mean for me? If his magic could heal Coop...No, I couldn't let myself go there. I did not need that kind of hope...and I did not want to have any kind of expectations from Raphael.

I'd always fantasized about living in a world where magic existed but I'd never really expected it to actually happen. I was at a loss about what to do with this newfound information. It didn't change the way I felt about Raph, that I was sure of, but it did fill me with a whole bunch of questions. What could

Raph do with his magic? Were there others like him? If mages existed, did other creatures like vampires and werewolves exist too?

The sound of a knock brought me out of my musings and I hurried over to the front door. Raphael smiled at me hesitantly when I opened the door, so I gave him a bright smile to tell him that nothing had changed between us. Yes, I had about a million questions for him. Yes, I was still in awe of what he was. But at the end of the day, Raphael was still the goofy, sweet guy I liked so much and nothing would change that for me, especially not this.

Visibly breathing a sigh of relief, he walked deeper into the room, Neya trailing in behind him. Hadn't we left her at his place when we left for the shelter? I didn't remember her being with us. Maybe Raph had stopped in at his place before coming here. I looked him over and my brows furrowed when I realized he was dressed in the same outfit as earlier.

I led Raph into the kitchen, waving over to the dining table. "Take a seat, the stew needs to well...stew for a bit more."

Raphael chuckled and ignoring my directions walked over to me, nudging my chin upwards. I met his green-brown eyes as he leaned closer and kissed me softly, his lips caressing mine with the gentlest of touches. I leaned into him automatically, hooking my arms around him as I pressed closer to him.

"I think you have some questions for me," Raph said after pulling away, a crooked smile on his face.

"So many questions!" I waved over to the chairs and this time, he took a seat, pulling me into the chair beside him. A warm feeling ran over the arm he was touching and I gasped. How had I never noticed this before? Now that I knew about it, I could so easily feel the warm tingle racing up my arm.

"You used your magic just now, didn't you?"

Raphael gave me an amused look as he said, "Yeah, it's almost a habit by now, sorry. Do you want me to stop?"

I shook my head vehemently. I'd felt healthier in the days since I met Raph than I had in my whole life. There was no way I would consciously decline that feeling. Not unless *he* wanted to stop. "No, not unless you want to. Is it tiring for you to do that for me?"

Raphael shook his head and squeezed my hand as he spoke, "I hate seeing you in pain and I'm glad I can help. It doesn't cost me too much energy, so we're all good."

I smiled at him, gratitude flowing through me before I let the questions fly. "What can you do with your magic? And where did you live before you came here? Are there others like you? And what about other supernatural creatures, do they exist too?"

Raphael's laughter stopped me from asking all the other questions that I had and my face warmed at my blabbering. I gave him a sheepish smile but didn't say anything as I waited for him to answer my questions.

"Okay, let me see. My magic comes from nature—which is why I have so many plants around my house—and until a few weeks ago, I thought it was useless since I couldn't heal like the rest of my family. But after meeting you, I realized my magic was just different. I lived at an island called Ravenshire. It's that island on the other side of the Silent Creek. The magic on the island keeps the humans from trying to reach it. I don't know how exactly it works, but you can only access the island through the portals in various cities that only mages know about. The island is full of mages so yes there are others like me, but everyone has different powers depending on their affinities. Vampires, werewolves, Fae...yes. Zombies and aliens, no."

"Wow, yeah, I see how that can be overwhelming. How about I get dinner while I process?" Mostly, I was still stuck on the first part of what he'd said and my mind was trying to lead me down a road I really didn't want to go down.

"I'll help," Raphael said, hopping to his feet and following me as I tried to wrap my mind around everything he'd told me. Gah, I could see now why the characters in the books always had such a hard time believing shit like this.

Raphael

Something was on Jai's mind. Well, I'd given him a lot to think about, so it was reasonable that he was lost in thought. He was quiet as we ate, too quiet. His silence was making me nervous. What if he decided he couldn't deal with all of this? I hadn't told him about our bond yet, but what if he rejected me before I could? I wished I could see what he was thinking, but mind reading wasn't a power I had. Even with our bond, it'd need to be a lot stronger for us to be able to send thoughts to each other, much less read each other's mind.

I played with my spoon as I tried to figure out what he was thinking. But the silence soon grew too much for me and I broke. "What are you thinking about?"

Jai looked up at me with wide eyes and then immediately blurted out, "What did you mean you'd thought your magic was useless?"

I winced, putting my spoon down as I chewed on my lip. The old taunts rang in my ears as I tried to gather my thoughts. I took a deep breath and tried my best to force the voices away. I wasn't useless anymore. Hell, I'd *never* been useless. I was different and no one had understood that before, me included. No one had thought that I could just be different. Now that I knew—or at the very least, suspected—what I could do, I knew I was probably more powerful than my parents. But it didn't matter anymore. I was done with them.

A small, warm hand wrapped around mine where I'd curled it into a fist on the table and I looked up to see Jai watching me with an encouraging smile. Blowing out a breath, I nodded my head and told him my story.

"I'm from a family of healers. Mages who can heal people with their magic," I explained. "My parents and my younger sister can heal almost anything from bullet wounds to burn victims. They can bring people back from the brink of death and I...I could never do that. In all the years I lived in Ravenshire, everyone told me I was useless, that I didn't deserve to be the part of such a powerful family. I didn't even have a semlee—a soul-bound animal, a companion that every mage has. Living there was...horrible. So a few weeks ago, I finally decided I'd had enough. I made up my mind to move here and live alone as a common human since I wasn't a competent enough mage."

My lips pulled into a smile as I thought about that day, the day I'd met Jai. "But then you literally stumbled into my life. I felt an instant connection to you, but it wasn't until the second time we met and I touched you that I realized how much you were hurting. Then I realized that I could heal you, that my powers worked on you and it was such a shock. You see, as powerful as my family is, they can't heal some stuff. Birth illnesses, disfigurement, cancer, that kind of stuff. But when I touched you, I realized I *could* heal you. Now I know that I do have magic, that I'm not useless. My powers are just different than what everyone has known healers to be capable of."

I stopped speaking at the consternation I could see growing on Jai's face. He'd pulled his hand back from where it had been covering mine and he sat straight in his chair, as if steeling himself against something awful. My brows furrowed as I tried to figure out what I'd said that would make him react like that. "What's wrong?"

"Are you...are you saying that I was some kind of experiment? Your guinea pig to see what your powers can do?"

"What?" I was honestly stumped for a moment because that was so far out of the blue I couldn't make heads nor tails of it. Once I realized he actually meant what he'd asked, I stumbled to my feet and walked over to his side, pulling him up and into a tight hug. I tipped his chin upwards so he was looking at me before I started speaking, "No, baby." I shook my head at just how crazy even the thought of Jai not being my everything was. I knew I'd need to tell him everything now to make him believe me. I'd hoped I would have some time before I'd need to tell him the rest of it, but I knew I needed to kill this thought in the bud. "Jai, you've read a lot of fantasy books, right? Do you know the concept of fated mates?"

Jai's big, brown eyes widened behind his glasses and he licked his upper lip as he nodded, something like hope shining in the soulful depths of his eyes.

I took a deep breath as I put my heart in his hands and the ball in his court. "Well, in the old language, a mate is called a Semnyar...and you are mine. I've known it for a while but obviously I couldn't tell you until now. You're the one fate picked for me, Jai and you already have my heart. You are my everything, not an experiment or a fling or anything like that. Meeting you was the best thing that ever happened to me. Yes, you helped me realize my magic wasn't useless, but that's not all you did. I haven't had a day since meeting you where I haven't smiled and it's all thanks to you. I know it's a lot to take in and that it would take you a long time to get where I'm at in regards to our relationship, but I'm not going anywhere, okay?"

"You're my...mate," Jai said, his voice barely above a whisper, his eyes wide as he stared up at me, lips parted invitingly. If I wasn't afraid he was about to freak out, I would've been pressing my lips to his.

"Are you going into shock? You're going into shock, aren't you?"

Jai laughed, a sweet, melodious sound that had me smiling in relief. He pressed closer to me, kissing the base of my collarbone as his arms tightened around my waist. "No, Angel. I'm not going into shock. Though yes, I do feel like I've stumbled into dreamland and all of this is going to disappear as soon as I wake up."

"It's not a dream, my sweet Semnyar. Can I call you that? Do you mind?"

"Do I mind a special nickname in a special language that only the two of us would know the meaning of?" Jai said, a teasing note to his voice and I laughed, my heart feeling warmer and fuller than it ever had. Jai knew everything and he wasn't freaking out. He wasn't afraid of me or what it meant to be my semnyar. He knew everything and he was still here. I could cry with relief.

Neya took that moment to scramble up my shoulder and nip insistently at my ear. "Oh, by the way, I should introduce you to my semlee, Neya."

Jai peeked up at Neya with wide eyes, a smile spreading across his lips. "Oh wow, this is seriously crazy. And awesome. It's crazy awesome and I'm getting way too overwhelmed. I think I need to sit down now." I should've known everyone had their limits, even someone as amazing and accepting as my semnyar. Mother, I couldn't stop thinking the words now that he knew everything. *My semnyar.*

"Hold on," I lifted Jai up into a bridal hold before carrying him over to the couch. I sat down, placing him on my lap and curling my arms around him.

Tucking his head into the crook of my neck, he mumbled, "You know I still have about a thousand more questions, right?"

I chuckled as I rubbed his back, sending wisps of my magic into his tired muscles. "I know, baby. I'll be right here when you wake up and we can continue, okay?" It was almost ten anyway, so I should've probably just carried him to bed but I really wanted to hold him like this for a bit, to revel in my semnyar's arms knowing he knew everything.

"I'm not that sleepy," Jai mumbled and I gave him a minute. As expected, he started snoring softly before the minute was up, his body relaxing into mine. I pulled him closer, burying my face in his dark hair and breathing in the coconut scent of his hair product. My semnyar was warm, comfortable and safe and that was all I needed.

THIRTEEN

Raphael

"So, tell me more about our bond, about being your semnyar," Jai said, his eyes closed. It was a few days since I'd told him about everything and he seemed to be taking everything pretty well. I was so glad. I'd been scared it would be too much for him, that he would decide staying with me was too much work. Even the thought of losing your semnyar was abhorrent to any supernatural being, and I didn't even want to think about what I'd do if Jai decided to leave me for some reason.

I turned on my side to face him and he mimicked my move, opening his eyes as his arm wrapped around my waist. The clouds had dispersed a bit today, so we'd decided to soak in some sun in my backyard. Padfoot and Neya were busy playing around as we lay on a blanket in the middle of the yard. I wished we could stay like this forever, surrounded by nature and holding each other.

Remembering the question Jai had asked, I smiled at him, running my fingers down his cheek in a gentle caress. His glasses were crooked since his face was smooshed against the blanket, so I folded my arm below my head and offered him my elbow.

With a sweet smile, he snuggled closer, resting his temple on my elbow so his glasses wouldn't be in the way. The move left us with barely a few inches between our lips and I had to force myself to think about his question so I wouldn't kiss him because I knew that once I started, I wouldn't be able to stop.

"The semnyar bond, right. Fate, who is basically the mother of all, knows everything. So she created the semnyar bond to tie together the souls she felt suited best together. She did it for every being, even humans. The thing is, non-humans are able to feel the bond while humans can't, which is why we actively look for our semnyar while humans only find theirs by pure luck unless their other half is a non-human. If you'd been non-human, we'd have known we belonged together the moment we first met."

"So...the people who find the love of their life and live their whole life with them...they're soul-mates?" Jai mused and I smiled in agreement, yet again surprised by how well he was taking everything. I think he would've been more surprised if I told him I used to be a Hollywood actor. Damn, I could show him my movies now, not that they'd been all that good. It would be fun to see what he thought of them, though.

"Exactly. Now, even though you are my semnyar, our bond isn't complete yet. Once it is, you'll gain my immortality, you won't have a mortal life span anymore. We'll also be able to sense each other, when we're close by, when the other is in pain, things like that."

Jai's eyes had widened when I started speaking and his mouth was open in an O of surprise. "You okay?"

"Um, did you just say I'll live forever?" His voice was hesitant, as if he didn't want to believe what I was saying.

Realization dawned just a little too late as I ran through what I'd said. Ugh, I should've eased him into that one. I knew how sensitive the topic of his illness was, and I should've known better than to throw it out there like that.

"Yeah. Even if something happens to me, you'll retain the immortality you gain from our bond," I murmured, rubbing my hand up and down his back comfortingly.

Jai gasped and his eyes filled with tears. "What? What's wrong, baby?"

He shook his head as I wiped the tears off and gave me a rueful smile. "Nothing. Just...I'd known from a young age that I wouldn't get to live a full life. Hell, my mom still tells everyone I'm a 'miracle' since I wasn't supposed to live past six months. So now, to hear I might get to live forever...it's just hard to believe, I guess."

Sometimes I forgot just how much my sweet semnyar had suffered in his short life. Twenty-three years spent thinking he'd never get to experience life fully...only to find out he'd live forever...I'd find it hard to believe too.

"You will, Jai. You'll get to live a long and healthy life. I can heal you, remember? Not just your aches and pains, but your heart and lungs too. It'll take a few months because it would require a lot of energy, but I promise you, you'll be completely healthy in a year or so."

Jai removed his glasses, placing them above his head and buried his face in the crook of my neck. He sniffled, his tears soaking into my hair. I rubbed his back in long, comforting strokes knowing this must be overwhelming to think about. Like he'd said the other day, for Jai this was like stepping into a dreamland and I knew he'd have a hard time believing it wasn't all going to disappear. I would just have to show him and let him experience it for himself.

Once he'd calmed down, he pulled away and gave me a sheepish smile. I wiped his cheeks and pecked his nose, making his smile widen.

"You know what I wanna do now?" Jai mumbled, a hopeful smile on his face as his eyes brightened with excitement. What was he up to now?

"What?"

"I'm going to make a list of all the things I'd always wished I could do. And I'm going to do them, hopefully with you by my side."

"I'll always be with you. What kind of things will you put on this wishlist of yours?"

"Wishlist. I like that. Hmm...the first one would be...learning how to ride a bike. It's kinda stupid to learn that now, though. Right? I already know how to drive a car. What would be the point of learning how to ride a bike?"

"Hey," I murmured, gripping his chin gently, "you don't need a reason to do anything, okay? We have forever now, we can do whatever we want."

Jai nodded slowly, processing my offer before looking up at me. "Can I..."

I gave him an encouraging nod and he continued, "Can I tell my brother about you? That you're a mage, I mean."

I chewed my lower lip as I mulled over his question. Telling him had been a no-brainer since he was my semnyar and no law would try to stop me from sharing everything with him. But his brother? I wasn't a hundred percent sure but I knew there was a clause that said I could tell my semnyar's family members a little about the supernatural world. Not everything, of course, but just enough so they know their kid is safe.

"You can't tell him everything. I'm sorry. I know I don't live in Ravenshire anymore, but I'm still bound by the laws, you know?"

"I understand, Angel. Just tell me what I can tell him."

"You can tell him I'm a mage and that I can heal you. I believe that would earn me a lot of cool points," I winked at him so he knew I was joking and he rolled his eyes at me.

"Got it. Let's hope he believes you."

"Yep, and if he doesn't, I'll just give him a demo," I told him with a wink.

"Is there another sick animal at the shelter?"

"Nope, I was thinking something like this," I said and using the inherent magic, I levitated some leaves over Jai's head in the shape of a crown. His eyes widened before a delighted laugh escaped his lips and he reached out to touch one of the leaves.

"Wow. Why didn't you show *me* something like this?"

"Um, because healing magic is more impressive? I don't know. I just didn't want you to think my magic was some kind of parlor trick." *Parlor tricks. Kiddo magic.* That's what the other mages had called my magic back in Ravenshire. If only they could see me now.

Jai nodded thoughtfully as he looked up at the crown. "I wish I could tell Cassian too. I don't like keeping secrets from the people I care about."

Cassian. He'd talked about this man before. He was Jai's best friend, wasn't he? "Who's Cassian?" I asked, just to make sure.

"Oh, he's my best friend. We haven't actually met, but he's a great guy. His pet, April, she's the biggest owl I've ever seen." Of course his best friend had a pet. And wait a minute...

"Wait. Is his last name Romanov?" I asked. It couldn't be him, right? The world couldn't really be such a small place?

Jai sat up, apparently tired of lying down and nodded. "How did you know that?"

I chuckled as I sat up and pushed Jai's glasses back on his face since he'd started squinting at me. "I don't think you need to worry about keeping secrets from him, Jai. Cassian Romanov is one of the most well-known mages in Ravenshire."

Jai gasped, his eyes widening comically. "He is? Is that why he never asked to meet? Have you met him?"

I shook my head even as a tinge of possessiveness shot through me. I was glad Cassian hadn't met my semnyar because well, he was mine.

"I haven't met him. He's kind of a hermit, actually. Lives in a stone mansion all by himself." And I couldn't fault him for that one. If I could've done that, I'd have a mansion of my own by now. Though I wouldn't go for a stone mansion. Those just gave me the creeps.

Jai frowned, his eyes darkening in sorrow over his friend. This was why I adored him. He cared so much about others. He was beautiful and I was so damn lucky to have him as my semnyar.

"He's usually so snarky when we chat, I had no idea he was so lonely," Jay murmured, his lips pulling down at the corners.

"Why don't we have a little fun with him then?" I asked, mostly in an attempt to cheer him up. I couldn't bear to see my semnyar sad and I could see his friendship with the fire-mage meant a lot to him, so I would try to keep my jealousy on the down low.

"What do you mean?"

"I don't know. Maybe tell him you know he's a mage but make it fun somehow?"

Jai got a scheming look in his eyes before he grinned at me and grabbed his phone from where he'd left it on the grass. I snuggled closer to him and leaned up so I could watch what he typed as he texted Cassian.

Jai: Hey Cass, I had the weirdest dream last night.

Cassian replied not a minute later, making us chuckle.

Cassian: Yeah? What about?

Jai: It was so weird. I saw you sitting on a throne in this huge stone mansion with April perched on your shoulder—

"Hey, you said mages have different kinds of magic, right? Do you know what Cassian's is?" Jai asked, looking up at me as his thumbs hovered over the screen.

"He's a fire mage," I told him and he continued typing.

—and you had ball of fire in your hand. You looked like a badass fire mage or something, I swear.

The three dots appeared for a moment before disappearing. Then it happened again. And again.

"I think you broke the man."

Jai chuckled as he watched the screen for another moment before shaking his head and hitting dial. "Hey, Cass."

I sat back and listened to the one-sided conversation, though it didn't look like Cassian got a chance to say much.

"Yeah so apparently I have a semnyar now. His name is Raphael. Woodward yeah. He told me about you when I mentioned you." I loved the blase way he said all of that, like it was no big deal that he'd suddenly found himself in this strange new reality.

Jai played with a lock of my hair, twirling it around his fingers as he listened to whatever Cassian said, nodding along. "Not much, honestly. Just that you're a hermit and a fire mage. Yeah, sure."

Jai pulled the phone away from his year before looking at me. "Hey Raph, Cassian wants to talk to you for a bit."

"Sure." I took the phone from him and pressed it to my ear as I sat up.

"Hello, Cassian. This is Raphael."

"Hello, Raphael. Congratulations on your bond."

"Thank you." A smile stretched across my lips as it did every time I thought about our bond.

"Um, I just wanted to ask you, could you please not tell Jai about my past? I like having one person in my life who doesn't think I'm a monster—Ow! Okay, I mean two people." I chuckled as I realized his semlee must have bitten him for his words and I was glad he had someone who cared, even if it was just his semlee.

"You know, I don't think that about you, either. What happened, it was an honest mistake. I promise I won't share your story with anyone, Cassian. It's yours to tell."

"Thank you," Cassian whispered, his voice thick with some unnamed emotion. "Tell Jai I'll text later, okay?" He'd ended the call before I could answer, so I handed the phone back to Jai.

"What was that about?"

I shook my head, giving Jai a sad smile. "Cassian's past...everyone in Ravenshire knows about it. So he was asking me not to tell you because he likes having one person who doesn't see him the same way everyone in Ravenshire does."

Jai nodded slowly, as if making sure he had his thoughts in order before he spoke, "I think that's exactly why we're so close, me and Cass. I was looking for a friend who looked past my illness and he was looking for one who looked past his well...past. Perfect match, right?"

I pouted, sticking my bottom lip out even further so I knew I looked comical. I wanted to make Jai smile again but I also didn't want him talking about him and Cass being a 'perfect match'. "We're the perfect match, my semnyar."

Jai grinned, shifting closer until our thighs were pressed together. "Aw, you don't like it when I talk about me and Cassian?"

I narrowed my eyes at him and he laughed, his worry over his friend disappearing as he moved closer, his arm curling around my neck as he pulled me into a kiss. I tasted the sunshine on his soft, warm lips and a moan escaped me as his other hand slid over my front, caressing me over the material of my shirt. I wanted to get rid of the clothes but I also wanted to take this slow. We'd have decades, maybe even centuries with each other, but we'd only get to experience the firsts once. I wanted to savor each and every one of our firsts.

When I pulled away, Jai's cheeks were warm under my palms. By now, it had become second nature to me to send some of my magic traipsing through him every few hours, healing any aches and pains he might be feeling. Jai sighed softly, his minty breath blowing over my face as his eyes fluttered close. "Thank you," he said softly and I quirked a brow even though he still had his eyes closed.

"What? For the kiss?"

Jai swatted my arm as he opened his eyes. "No, you crazy man. Thank you for coming into my life and making it so much more beautiful."

I blushed at the intensity in his gaze and pulled him into another kiss because he was my semnyar and I couldn't resist his sweet charm.

FOURTEEN

Jai

Saturday had me unable to sit still as I waited for Joy to get here with his bike. I hadn't told him much on the phone, just ordered him to come over with his bike. He'd been understandably confused, but he'd promised me he'd be here, just like I'd expected him to. I wondered if he'd believe my claims. I wondered what he'd say when I told him I would be living a long, healthy life like him.

"You're really eager for this, aren't you?' Raphael asked from where he leaned against the back of my couch, watching me as I peeked out the window to check if Joy was here yet.

"Yeah. It's just another thing that made me different, you know? My doctor told my parents that I shouldn't do anything that would make me strain myself so my parents just decided to treat me like a china doll. I don't fault them for it, obviously, but there are a lot of things I never got to do because of it." Like learning to ride a bike, going hiking, riding a roller coaster...gods, the list was endless. So many missed outings with friends, summer camps...I'd missed out on a lot when I was a kid.

Raphael walked over to me, a pensive look on his face that had my brows furrowing as he took my hands in his. "What's wrong?" The question popped out of my mouth unbidden and I waited for him to answer. Raphael looked the best with a wide smile brightening up his face.

"Nothing is wrong. I just wanted to say that if you get tired or are in pain, I'll definitely help you. But...well, if you fall down and get hurt, my magic would be useless." The shame in his voice had me straightening up, anger flowing through me at the thought of all the people who had made him feel like that over the years. He'd told me his true age—and I was still having a little trouble processing *that*—and I couldn't imagine living that long with people telling you you're useless and not believing it. But Raph was so far from useless and I *needed* him to see that. I didn't know if it was the mate bond talking or that was just how strongly I felt about this, but suddenly I needed Raph to see how good and perfect he was. How much he meant to me.

I pulled my hands away from his and took his face between my palms, tilting my head up so I was looking right into his green-brown eyes. "Listen to me, Raph. You are not useless. Fuck all those people who made you think so, it was their loss that they didn't figure out just how amazing you are. Their loss and my gain, alright? You are beautiful and amazing and I'm not even talking about your magic when I tell you that you are the most important thing in my life now. I know it's quick, and maybe it's because of our bond, but I know you belong with me and I with you. Promise me you will never think that of yourself ever again."

The whole time I'd spoken, Raphael had watched me with this wide eyed gaze, as if he couldn't believe what I was saying. Now, he took a deep, shuddering breath and nodded, blinking slowly as if trying to make sure he remembered every word. Then he was pulling me closer to him and leaning down, claiming my lips with his.

This kiss was different from all the kisses we'd shared since we started dating. This kiss wasn't gentle or sweet. It was intense, with our bodies pressed together, molding into each other as we traded moans and touches and our tongues danced together. The feeling was exquisite, the aroma of freshly cut grass and honey thick around me, making me feel almost dizzy with want. I'd never felt so turned on so quickly before, and my fingers tangled in Raph's hair, pulling him even closer—if that was even possible.

"Ew, gross guys," Joy's voice broke us apart and I trained my eyes on a spot behind Raph as I tried to control my breathing so I wouldn't jump on him in front of my little brother. I also didn't want to scar Joy with a sight he didn't need in his life. Once I'd calmed down enough that I wouldn't flash him, I turned to face him, though I stayed close to Raph.

"Sorry, I was just surprised," Joy mumbled, his cheeks flaming red as he looked everywhere but at us.

"It's okay."

"So, what's the bike for?"

"Hmm?" It took me a minute to process his question and then remember what the plan was. Raph had scrambled my brain good. "Oh, right. Well, before we get to that I need to tell you something. And I need you to keep an open mind."

Joy quirked a brow at me before his eyes flitted between the two of us, widening with every flick. "Don't tell me you're moving in together or something."

"What? No!" Though I couldn't say with certainty that the idea wasn't appealing. That was too quick though, right? Then again, I didn't know what the rules were for fated mates or *semnyars* as Raph called them.

"Cool. Because that would be way too fast. So what is it?"

I shared a glance with Raph and he gave me an encouraging nod and a sweet smile, his swollen lips catching my attention and holding it until Joy cleared his throat. Loudly.

I shook off the urge to kiss Raph again and turned back to face my brother. "Open mind, okay? You're probably going to think I'm crazy but I need you to see, okay?"

Joy's face scrunched up in confusion and I had a moment of doubt. What if he didn't believe me? Or what if he thought Raph was a freak? What if he told someone?

"Before I tell you, I need you to promise me you won't tell anyone."

Joy straightened up, his eyes flashing as he looked at me and then Raph and then back to me. "Is he hurting you or something?"

I rolled my eyes at him even as my heart warmed at how he wanted to protect me, even if it was supposed to be the other way around.

"No, *chhote*. Raph is awesome." I chewed on my lower lip before blurting out. "And he's a mage. He can do magic, healing magic to be specific."

"What?" Joy asked, and I knew he didn't believe me. Not yet. Of course he didn't. *He* didn't spend all his time reading books with magic and wishing magic was real.

"Raph?" I asked him without looking away and then a moment later, leaves from my backyard were around us, flitting through the air like tiny birds.

"Woah!" Joy exclaimed and I grinned at the awe and excitement on his face. No fear, thank the gods. "What kinda trick is this?"

Joy looked at me with wide eyes and I shook my head. "Joy," I whispered, walking closer, "It's not a trick. It's real magic. And Raph...Raph can...he can *heal* me. Like, everything."

Joy's eyes widened further, lighting up with something akin to hope as he looked at Raph. He opened his mouth but no words came. Shaking his head, he tried again, his voice thick, "You can?"

Raph nodded as he walked closer, slipping his arms around me as he hugged me from behind. "I can. It will take a few months, but Jai will be completely healthy at the end of it. And he's my soulmate, so I'd never let anything happen to him." I leaned into Raph as he spoke but I kept my eyes on Joy. He looked like he was starting to believe us, though his brows were still furrowed.

"Soulmate? Like that fated mates stuff from your books?" Joy asked me and I nodded.

Joy nodded, then nodded again and it was only now that I realized he was shaking. I shrugged out of Raph's arms and pulled my brother closer. He sank into me and I could feel his body shaking as he clung to me. Even though he was taller and bigger than me, all muscles to my all bones, in this moment I was the big brother comforting my little one.

I rubbed his back gently as he shuddered. "Hey, we're okay. What's wrong?"

He pulled back after a few moments, rubbing his face with his palms before giving me a sheepish smile. "Sorry, *bhai*. I've kind of always known that you might not be around forever, you know? So I guess it was kind of overwhelming—good overwhelming, 'course—when I realized I get to keep my big bro. Gods, I was so scared. But this is real? You'll really be okay?"

I nodded, squeezing his shoulders as I spoke, "Yeah, I believe Raph. You know how much I avoid any kinds of false hopes when it comes to this, right? But I believe him, Joy. I've seen him work his magic and I've felt what it does to me. I'll be okay. We'll be okay."

It was the first time my brother had ever told me how my illness affected him beside the small things. He'd never been angry when his plans had to be canceled because of me or when my parents picked me over him. I'd never even realized he thought about what could happen in the future. Damn, I was pretty self-centered, wasn't I?

"I'm not going anywhere, *chhote*. Don't you worry."

Joy smiled at me now, a bright and huge smile that lit up his face. Then he turned to Raphael and with the excitement of a seventeen year old, he asked, "So what all can you do with your magic?"

Three hours later, we were finally standing on the street outside my house, with me straddling the bike and Joy giving me directions. If I had been healthy, I would've been the one who taught him when he was a kid, but oh well. At least we got to share this experience, even if it was the other way around.

It wasn't actually as difficult as I'd expected it to be, and I was able to stop myself from crashing every time the bike started tilting, so I didn't even get hurt. On my eleventh attempt—yes, I kept a count—I finally found my balance and biked to the end of the street, laughing the whole way as the wind whipped my face, making me squint through my glasses. I knew I wasn't going as fast as it felt like to me, but I was riding a bike and that was something to be happy about because I'd never expected I would get to.

I had to use my legs to turn the bike around once I reached the end of the street. The way back to my place was slightly uphill, so I was panting and gasping by the time I reached Raphael, though I was still grinning like a loon.

As soon as I got off the bike, I stumbled and Raph was there to catch me, his hands warm around me. I closed my eyes as I felt his magic wash over me—I'd gotten better at sensing it now that I knew it was there—and I sighed as I felt the burn in my lungs, my legs and my arms disappear.

I opened my eyes, feeling better than I had when I started biking and turned to find Joy watching us with a bright smile on his face. "It really works, doesn't it?" He asked, his voice full of wonder.

I nodded as I linked my fingers with Raph's, shooting him a wink before turning back to look at Joy. "Come on in, I'll make us all dinner."

"You really aren't tired at all?"

I shook my head with a smile and Joy looked so absolutely delighted as he raced into the house ahead of us.

The whole time I made dinner—and then afterward while we ate said dinner—Joy asked Raph question after question after question. Some of the questions he asked were ones I'd been meaning to ask myself, so I listened intently as they talked, though I didn't interrupt. Joy asked about Raph's magic and cooed over Neya when he realized who and what she was. I noticed that Raph dodged questions about his family and Ravenshire most of the time, but other than that he answered every question Joy had.

Watching the two of them together warmed my heart to no end and I was glad I didn't need to hide this truth from Joy. But how would I tell my parents? I wasn't sure if telling them about Raph's magic would be a good idea. My dad was an extremely rational person and believed only in science while my mom believed in all the Indian gods and deities. Though she also believed in black magic. What if she thought Raph's magic was evil? Also, did black magic actually exist? I'd have to ask Raphael.

Either way, I didn't know if telling them would be the best idea, but I would need to figure something out, right? They'd see the changes in my reports when I started getting better, so I needed to tell them something.

It was late by the time Joy left with directions to not tell anything to our parents just yet. He left his bike with me so I could practice if I wanted to. Once he was gone, I walked into the kitchen to help Raph with clean-up. He was just finishing up loading the dishwasher and turned to me when he heard me approaching.

"Will you stay tonight? Just to cuddle and sleep?" I wasn't a hundred percent sure why I wanted to go slow. A part of me knew Raph wouldn't leave me, not when I was his mate. But then again, I couldn't really feel the bond, so sometimes it didn't feel real to me. I wanted to savor what we had. After all, if what Raph had said was true, we would live forever. And we would only get to experience our firsts once. So why not drag it out as much as possible? We had all the time in the world now.

Raphael seemed to be on the same page as me because he never pushed for more either and I was glad for that. He smiled widely now, stepping into my space and curling his arms around me. I sank into the embrace, feeling warm and cared for and *home*.

Huh. Maybe I *could* feel the bond after all.

Raphael

The next two months passed by in a bliss and I still found it hard to believe I'd been lucky enough to have Jai as my semnyar. He was everything I could've ever asked for. He needed me to take care of him and in return he made me feel like I mattered. For the first time in my life, I had someone who saw me for who I was, who cared about me and not how much power I had. Yes, my magic helped Jai and was important to him, but he'd always made it clear to me that I was more important than my magic to him.

Jai's monthly hospital visits showed us that my magic was helping him, truly helping him. The pressure on his lungs had decreased just a bit and with steady healing, he'd be able to stop taking his medicines in a month or so. I knew the thought was a bit incomprehensible to him at the moment. There had never been a day in his life that he hadn't needed his medicines, and they were as much a part of his life as food and water were. But soon, he wouldn't need them anymore.

I'd gone with him to the hospital on his last visit—after meeting his mom and assuring her I'd take care of him—and introduced myself to his doctor. Humans didn't know about the existance of mages—unless they were a mages' semnyar like Jai was mine—but the doctors in all the major hospitals around Mistvale knew about the Woodward family and their special capabilities when it came to healing patients. They believed we were such gifted and good at what we did, but I was pretty sure they suspected we weren't normal.

I'd told Jai's doctor what he meant to me and assured him I'd heal him. He'd offered me a job at the hospital once he realized the kind of illnesses I could heal and I'd told him I would think about it once Jai was completely healed. My powers weren't strong enough to work with multiple people and Jai came first for me, always.

We'd also figured out a way to keep my involvement on the down low from Jai's parents. Instead, Dr. Merryweather would be telling them that he was starting a new treatment on Jai. It was for the best because Jai wasn't sure if his science loving father and slightly superstitious mother would be understanding of what I could do.

I hadn't thought much of it when I told the doctor who I was, and I'd forgotten all about the visit after a few days. I'd forgotten who else worked at the hospital and I really, *really* shouldn't have.

FIFTEEN

Jai

The dog park wasn't as crowded as I'd expected it to be this fine evening, but I was glad for it. I never was one for crowded places. Staying home most of the time for one reason or another had turned me into an introvert a long time ago. Or maybe I'd have been an introvert regardless of the way I grew up. Either way, I preferred staying at home than going out, unless it was with Raphael, of course.

The sun was on its downward climb, peeking through the clouds that were a permanent presence now that it was late December. Christmas was in a few days, though neither of us celebrated it; Raph because it wasn't something mages celebrated and me because I was more likely to celebrate Diwali since neither of my parents were Christian. My dad was an atheist and my mom Hindu, so the festivals I did celebrate were all from my mom's culture. I loved celebrating her festivals too because there were so many and they had such a variety.

Padfoot shot off to run laps around the park as soon as I unclipped his leash and I laughed as he engaged another dog—a golden retriever who was just a bit smaller than my baby—into playing a game of tag with him.

"Thanks for coming with me," I murmured as I tangled my fingers with Raphael's and looked up at him.

He gave me his usual cheery, slightly crooked smile, his blond hair almost glowing in the warm sunlight. He was dressed in a red hoodie and tight denims that showed off his lean muscles and I had to force myself to keep my eyes on his face.

"I wouldn't want to be anywhere else," he replied and the sincerity I heard in his voice had me smiling. I'd never imagined I'd get to feel this and even after almost three months together, it still felt like a dream sometimes. I'd always hoped but never believed that I'd get to walk hand in hand with my boyfriend and dream about a future. I'd never even let myself believe that I *had* a future. Then again, until a few months ago, that had been the truth.

But now, I knew magic was real. I knew Raphael had magic that could heal me, that could make me whole again, and give me a future. A future with him.

I also knew that even if he didn't have the magic, I'd like him just as much. The only difference would've been that I would've avoided my feelings because of my no dating rule. But I didn't have to fear the future—or lack thereof—now, right?

"Ow!" Raphael's loud shout had me pulling out of my thoughts and looking around for Padfoot. He was nowhere near us and I realized he hadn't slammed into Raph like I'd thought he had.

"What? What is it?" I asked when I saw that Raph was holding his free hand over his eye.

"Something in my eye," he answered with a pitiful whimper.

"Let me see." I pulled at his arm until he uncovered his eye and slowly flicked it open. Whatever had hurt him was too small to see, so I leaned up on my toes, placing my palms on both sides of his face to hold him steady and blew on his slightly red eye.

His eyelid flickered as he tried to keep it open and I blew on his eye once more, a gentler puff of air meant to sooth his eye.

"Okay?" I asked him, hoping the fleck had escaped. He could try washing it out, I supposed. That might work, right?

"I'm okay. It's gone, whatever it was," Raphael said, giving me a sheepish smile as if he expected me to tease him for it.

"That's good." I leaned up again and gave him a chaste kiss before pulling away. I let one of my hands drift downward before tangling my fingers with Raph's.

"Sorry, I get weird when something touches my eyes. How about we go play with Pads for a bit?" He offered and I grinned at him as I nodded. I got a feeling he'd only get more flustered if I lingered on the topic of his eye. I didn't know why he was so flustered about it anyway. We all had our quirks, our fears and things that made us go ew.

I played tag with Padfoot and Raph—another thing that wouldn't have been possible three months ago—and I laughed as Padfoot chased me, surprised at how much better I already felt. Raph had said it would take a few months before I was perfectly healthy, but even now I felt so much better than I had in years.

We played until the sun had set and only when my stomach started grumbling did we stop. The park wasn't far from our house, so once Raph had kissed me—and used the kiss as an excuse to send some of his magic seeping into me—I snapped Padfoot's leash into place and led us home, Neya racing in from wherever she'd disappeared off to and situating herself on Raph's shoulder.

I breathed in the cool evening breeze and tasted the rain in the air. My favorite thing about Mistvale—and what an appropriate name *that* was—was how much it rained here. I loved rain. I loved the sound of the raindrops pitter-pattering on my roof and I loved how the world looked after a bout of rainfall, bright, clean and new.

Raphael's phone rang just as we stepped into my place and I unclipped Padfoot's leash as I walked into the kitchen to get us some water, giving Raph privacy to take his call.

"No," Raph snapped, his voice so uncharacteristically harsh that I found myself walking back into the living room. Raph stood near the couch, his free hand curled into a fist while he pressed the phone to his ear with the other. His lips were pressed into a thin line, his green-brown eyes blazing with anger...and hurt. I'd never seen him like this. He almost looked like a completely different person than the man I knew. The man I'd come to lo...His eyes fell on me and he extended his free hand to me, a desperate look on his face I'd never seen before.

I walked over to him and took his hand, holding it tightly as I pressed myself to him in an attempt to comfort him. Who was calling him? Who was hurting my beautiful angel? I'd never been a particularly confrontational person—can't really do that when you might start gasping for breath in the middle of a rant—but right now all I wanted to do was take the phone from Raph and give a few choice words to the person who was hurting him.

"Stop it, mother," Raphael's voice broke as he spoke the words and I dropped his hand so I could curl my arms around him and hold him to me. His arm held me tighter to him as he continued speaking, "For years you've told me how useless

I am and now when you find out about my powers suddenly you want me back? Well, guess what? I hate the bigoted people who live in Ravenshire. And I absolutely hate the fact that my own mother only wants me now that she can show everyone she didn't give birth to a useless piece of shit. I don't care for your love, mother. I've spent way too long begging for it. I'm done."

Raphael took a huge, shuddering breath and I pressed my lips to the base of his collar bone, hoping to soothe him with the touch. I'd known his relationship with his parents wasn't the best, but he'd never talked about it. How could someone not be proud of someone as lovely and amazing as Raph? Even without his magic, Raphael was the most beautiful person I'd ever met, outside and inside.

"I've finally found someone who cares about me. I matter to someone and it's not you. It should've been you. I hope you realize that someday. Please don't contact me again. Goodbye." Raphael slumped into me the moment the call ended, and all I could do was hold him as he buried his face in the crook of my neck and let himself go.

Raphael

I couldn't believe her nerve. After all the taunts, all the times she'd asked me all those awful questions. *Why can't you just try a bit harder? Do you know what people say about you? About me?* After all of that, she still had the guts to call me and ask me to come back now that *I've finally found my powers*. My power. That was all she had ever cared about. She was my mother and all she had ever cared about was how many golden stars I could add to her reputation.

My mind kept playing the conversation on repeat, as if hearing her words again and again would help me. I wished I'd checked the called ID before I picked up the call, but I'd been so caught up in Jai that I'd barely glanced at the phone.

I shuddered as I heard her voice again, cold and distant and so different from the way she was with my sister. My sister was perfect, after all. Why wouldn't she love her?

"Hello, son," she'd said, as if nothing had happened, as if I hadn't left her damned house because of the way she'd treated me. She'd kept speaking even as it had taken me a moment to catch up to the fact that my mother was calling me. More than three months since I'd left Ravenshire and she called me a couple of weeks after I visited the hospital. What gives? "I heard at the hospital that you've finally discovered your powers. I think it's time you came back to Ravenshire, isn't it?"

"No," I'd snapped at her even as my heart had broken when I realized she was exactly as I'd thought her to be. A part of me—the stupid little boy who still wished his mom would love him—had still held on to the hope that she would come around, that she would tell me that my powers didn't matter, that I was still her son. But I'd been wrong, because power did matter. It was all that mattered to her.

Well, fuck her and fuck Ravenshire. I didn't remember everything I'd told her as the anger and hurt had consumed me, but I knew I'd never, ever be talking to her again. I was done with her. I was done with the whole mother-damned island.

I had my semnyar and my semlee. I had the power to make my semnyar healthy again. I didn't need them. I didn't need any of them.

As I came back to myself, I realized I was lying on Jai's couch, or more accurately, in his lap. My head rested on his chest and my tears had soaked into his t-shirt. My arms were tight around his waist, my legs between his. I freed one hand to wipe away my tears, embarrassed at how completely I'd broken down in front of him. Weak. I was so fucking weak.

I didn't meet his eyes, couldn't bring myself to but then his fingers had a hold of my chin and he turned my head so I was facing him. His brows were furrowed in concern and he ran the fingers of his free hand through my hair, brushing it away from my face. "You okay?"

I licked my lips, my throat dry from all the crying and nodded.

"I know I'm not really strong and I'd probably end up with broken fingers, but I want to punch everyone who ever treated you badly."

I shook my head, a reluctant smile gracing my lips as I imagined the scenario. "I'm sorry. I overreacted."

"No." Jai's voice was firm and I looked up at him as he continued speaking, "Never apologize for what you feel, Angel. From what I heard, your parents are pieces of shit and I can't imagine what living with them was like. But I also know that it hurts worse when the people who are supposed to love you don't. You shouldn't need to earn their love and they don't get to say they love you now when they've hurt you all your life. Your feelings are valid, okay?"

I nodded, too overwhelmed to say anything. "How about I order some pizza and we just cuddle for a bit?" Jai offered and as always, he knew exactly what I needed. I needed my semnyar to hold me and remind me that I was his. That I mattered to him. That he wouldn't give up on me like everyone else had.

I nodded again, pressing my lips to his chest in thanks. My semnyar knew what was best for me and I was so damn lucky to have him in my life.

After a dinner of pizzas on the couch, I changed into my sleep clothes—we each had a bunch of clothes at the other's place since we stayed over so often now—and climbed into the bed beside Jai who immediately pulled me closer.

Even though I was taller than him, today I got to be the little spoon. Jai pulled me closer to his front and I slid down enough so my head was tucked under Jai's chin, his arm wrapped tightly around my chest.

I stared at the bed covers as I opened my mouth to tell him how good this felt, but instead what came out of my mouth was, "I wish my mom was more like yours."

"Oh, Angel..." Jai murmured before turning me around so I was facing him. I didn't want to meet his eyes though, didn't want him to see the tears in mine, so I buried my face in his chest, wrapping my arms tightly around him and tucking one leg over his hip.

I didn't know where the tears had come from. I'd thought I'd spent all the tears I had for my parents. After all, my mom had been the same for as long as I've lived. I'd always known she only saw my powers—or lack thereof—when she saw me. Why was it hitting me so hard now? Why did I care?

"Why does it hurt so much, Jai? I'd always known she didn't love me. So why am I feeling like this?"

Jai ran his fingers through my hair, and even though he wasn't a healer, he was my semnyar and his touch comforted me and made me feel loved, everything I'd always wanted. Someone to hold me on my bad days. Someone to love me for who I was.

"Angel, we all want to be loved. And our moms are supposed to be the one person who loves us unconditionally. I know you've known how she feels about you for some time now, but I think a part of you still hoped that she would love you regardless. I guess today's call just made you realize that she is a selfish bitch and doesn't deserve your love." Jai gasped softly, his hands tightening around me before he continued, "I'm so sorry. I know I shouldn't speak badly of her-"

"No, you're right," I said, cutting him off. I pulled away from his chest and looked up at him. I knew I was probably a sight for sore eyes with my tangled hair and red eyes, but all I could see in Jai's eyes was concern and care. For me. "You're right, semnyar. My mom's a selfish woman and I shouldn't let her hurt me. Not anymore. I have you and Neya and Padfoot. You're all I need."

Jai smiled that soft smile of his before leaning down and kissing me. My lips were soft from crying and Jai's tongue kept returning to them for a taste. He pulled away after a minute of lazy, lovely kissing and rested his chin on top of my head. "You also have my ma, dad and Joy, alright? We're forever, right? So they're your family too."

I nodded, letting the comfort of his words and his arms around me seep into me. My eyes fluttered shut and Jai snuggled closer. My head returned to its nook beneath Jai's chin and I breathed in his sweet, chocolate scent and finally let myself fall into slumber, safe in the arms of the man I loved.

SIXTEEN

Jai

I woke up early the next morning to find Raph wrapped around me like a koala, much like he'd been when we'd fallen asleep last night. My heart hurt for him, for the pain I'd seen in his eyes, the pain I'd *felt* in my own heart. I didn't know if that was because of the bond or because I just loved him so much, but I'd hurt for him as if it was my own pain.

As I watched his eyelids flutter in his sleep, the long lashes resting against his cheek, still a bit tear stained from last night, I decided I needed to do something special for him. Something to cheer him up and show him that he was loved. I didn't want to say the words just yet, but I could definitely show him.

I grabbed my phone to check my schedule, careful not to wake Raph. I had a few articles to write and a website to design this week, but I'd probably be able to get them done if I stayed up for a bit tonight. It wasn't like I did most of my work during the day anyway, so I put my phone away and after a lot of shifting and freezing so Raph wouldn't wake up, I finally managed to escape from his arms.

I brushed my teeth and did my business quickly—and quietly—before heading into the kitchen. I made some tea and choco-chip pancakes since they were Raph's favorite before setting everything up on a tray along with more chocolate syrup.

Giving Padfoot his own food so he wouldn't try to eat ours, I headed back into the bedroom, smiling when I found Raphael still asleep and splayed over the whole bed. I placed the tray on the bedside table before crawling onto the bed and kneeling between his legs.

We hadn't gone farther than making out and some heavy petting, but the sight of his morning wood and the need to make him feel appreciated and adored had me leaning over and pressing a kiss to his lips. He mumbled in his sleep, his arms curling around me as he kissed me lazily. I knew he wasn't fully awake yet, so I pulled away, trailing kisses down his jaw until I reached the crook of his neck. There, I feasted. I licked at his skin, tasting the salt of his sweat and the delicious, slightly grassy taste of him. Was that a mage thing? Did he taste and smell like grass because he was connected to nature?

I licked and sucked, smiling against his skin when he moaned. Oh, he was definitely awake now. I didn't let up, though. Instead, I trailed kisses down his chest, glad he'd gone to bed shirtless. His pale pink nipples had turned into hard nubs that I licked at with my tongue, making him moan again. I loved the sound of his breathy, sexy moan and I nipped at his nub just to hear it again.

When I reached the waistband of his sleep pants, I looked up at him, a question in my eyes. The look on his face, the flushed cheeks and hooded eyes, had me leaking in my own pants. But this was about him, so I ignored my own hard on as I pulled his pants off, smiling at the wet spot I found on his briefs.

I had to move away to pull the pants and underwear off him, but I couldn't get back between his legs fast enough. His cock, long and lean like the rest of him was hard, pulsing and so gorgeous as it rested against his stomach, bobbing with every panting breath he took. I couldn't wait for the day I'd get to feel him inside me.

I knelt between his legs and trailed my finger oh-so-slowly up his cock, making him shudder. "Jai, please!"

I winked at him before leaning forward and running my tongue from the base of his cock to the tip as lightly as I could, chuckling when he whimpered. Giving in to both our desires, I covered the head of his cock with my mouth and we both moaned. His salty deliciousness had me humping against the mattress in a desperate attempt to feel some friction. I'd never done this before but that didn't mean I was completely useless. I'd read way too much fiction on the art of blowjobs to not be at least passably good.

I suckled on the tip for a bit, enjoying the drops of precum that leaked out of his slit before pushing forward. I swallowed him down, my hands holding on to his hip to stop him from pushing forward as I took him in all the way until my nose was buried in his nicely trimmed pubic hair. I breathed in his musky, slightly sweaty scent as I swallowed around him.

"Holy shit, Jai. That feels amazing," Raph groaned and I pulled back before plunging forward again and again and again until Raph was a desperate, writhing mess underneath me.

I trailed my right hand down his hip before taking his balls into my palm. I massaged them slowly as I used my other hand to pump him, pulling back so I could play with his slit with my tongue.

"I'm gonna..." Raph started to say but he didn't need to finish because his salty essence filled my mouth as he trembled around me and I swallowed every salty drop, licking and kissing his tip until he was whimpering from being overstimulated.

I crawled up his body, trailing kisses as I went before claiming his lips with mine. I couldn't stop myself from rubbing my hardness—still trapped in my sleep pants—against his abs as I kissed him, his tongue delving into my mouth to taste his own cum. I shuddered in his arms as I came, my arms tightening their grip around him as I tucked my face into the crook of his neck and breathed in his scent as the aftershocks trembled through me.

"Holy shit," Raph mumbled against the top of my head and I chuckled, kissing the hickey I'd left there before pulling away to look into his bright eyes. I was so happy to see the sated, slightly loopy smile on his face that I couldn't resist flicking his nose. His face scrunched up adorably, forcing me to press forward and claim his lips into another, much softer kiss.

As I came down from my high, the icky situation in my pants let itself be known and I pulled back with a sigh. "Let's clean up. I brought you breakfast in bed but then I decided I needed to have you for breakfast. So now we'll be having cooled down pancakes."

Raphael blushed prettily and my heart warmed, both at this sweet, shy side of him and the fact that he'd let me see it.

After we'd both cleaned up, I led him back to the bed where I placed the tray between us and gestured for him to start eating. After all, it was his favorite and I'd never been much of a breakfast eater anyway, so I'd probably eat whatever he couldn't finish.

As I watched Raphael lick the chocolate syrup off his fingers, I realized that I needed to tell him how I felt.

Why the hell was I waiting anyway? I knew better than most people how easily things could go wrong, how short life could be. Did I really want to risk something happening without me getting the chance to tell Raph how I felt? Without telling him how amazing he was, how much I loved him? Sure, we'd only known each other for three months, but we were semnyars, so of course I already loved him, right? What was not to love?

"I love you," I blurted out and Raph looked up at me with wide eyes, his hand still raised up to his mouth which now hung open.

"Excuse me, what?"

I smiled at his adorably surprised face and leaned forward to wipe some of the syrup off the corner of his mouth with my thumb before licking it. "I said, I love you."

His mouth moved as if he wanted to say something and then his eyes flooded with tears, but unlike last night his eyes only seemed to shine brighter as they did. "R-really? You're not just saying that to make me feel better, are you?"

I shifted closer to Raph and pushed the tray away. Kneeling up, I held his face between my palms and met his unique, green-brown eyes. Eyes that showed me he felt the same without him having to say a word. Eyes that had held me captive since the moment I first saw them. "I love you, my sweet angel. You've brought nothing but joy and happiness into my life from the moment I met you. I love you. I'll love you even if you lose your magic tomorrow and I'll love you forever if I am lucky enough to spend it with you. I love you, Raphael Woodward."

A tear slid down Raph's cheek and I wiped it away with my thumb before leaning up and kissing him. His lips were soft and sweet from the chocolate and I kissed them slowly, cherishing the fact that I had him. He was perfect. My other half in every way. I was so fucking lucky to have him and I would do everything in my power to show him that every single day of our very long lives.

I tasted the chocolate on his tongue as I delved deeper and he melted in my arms, sinking into me as if it took all his energy to hold himself up even that much.

When I pulled away, his cheeks were wet, but the wide smile on his lips said they were happy tears. "I love you too, Jai Presley. Not just because you're my semnyar, but because you see the real me, because you love Padfoot like he's your own kid, because you're so fucking strong and no one has ever loved me the way you do."

I smiled, leaning up to peck his nose because I couldn't resist those adorable freckles before pulling away. "Finish eating. I've got plans for us."I watched his face light up with excitement as he pulled the tray back to him and resumed eating. I watched him eat as I sipped the lukewarm tea and smiled, feeling warm, happy and more free than I ever had. I was with my other half and he loved me like I loved him. I had my fur baby and my soulmate and a long future ahead of me. What more could I want?

SEVENTEEN

Jai

The day was surprisingly warm after the week of rain we'd had and I couldn't stop turning my face towards the sky every once in a while to soak up the few, gentle rays of sunshine that managed to sneak through the cover of clouds.

I'd decided to make use of the good weather to scratch off another activity from my wishlist: hiking. Well, I'd mostly wanted to spend time with Raphael and I would be just as happy sitting at home and cuddling on the couch with him, but now that I didn't get tired every five minutes, I wanted to experience all the things I'd never been able to. Like hiking.

Admittedly, neither of us had any knowledge about hiking and Mistvale didn't even have a *hill,* so working with what we did have, we'd decided to take a long walk through the Silent Creek Park, which was so dense and full of flora that we wouldn't be wrong in calling it a mini-jungle. It was unlike any park I'd ever been to, with trees so huge they almost blocked out the sky. The trees themselves were ones I'd never seen before, with trunks that twisted around each other and yet managed to look beautiful and leaves the size of my palm hanging off of spindly branches covered in moss.

Raphael told me the reason this park was so...magical was because of its closeness to Ravenshire, the island Raphael came from and the one that housed a good number of the mages in the world. Raphael didn't talk about the people of Ravenshire much, but from what little he'd told me I'd gotten the feeling that though he'd adored the island, the people there had made it difficult for him to stay in love with the place.

All the residents of Ravenshire were mages and though most of them came over to Mistvale for work, there were apparently portals around the city that led them back home at the end of the day. Raphael said that humans couldn't access the island, that the moment they tried, they'd be distracted by some or the other thought and forget all about it. It was some old magic the founder of Ravenshire had put in place to keep the existence of mages a secret and it seemed to be working well.

Ravenshire was a mystery to me and I yearned to ask Raphael more about it. I mean, it was a magical island! Of course I wanted to know all about it! The only reason I wasn't hounding Raph with questions about the place was that every time he talked about his home, he got this sad, slightly homesick look on his face and I *hated* it. Raphael looked best with a smile on his face and I didn't want to do anything to take that smile away from his face, curiosity be damned.

I looked around as we walked, Neya and Padfoot leading the way a few paces ahead of us, and tried to imagine what Ravenshire looked like if just the proximity to the island made this park look so beautiful. The moss covered tree trunks around us reminded me of the color of Raphael's eyes and I could easily imagine him amongst these trees, lounging on one of the branches with a hoard of tiny animals around him. I'd always been good with animals, but Raph's ease with them put mine to shame.

If this was what being close to magic did to a place, I could only imagine what living with magic must do to it. Ravenshire must be full of greenery and lush plants and huge trees, right? If only I could ask Raphael. But I wouldn't. My curiosity didn't warrant making him sad. He'd told me enough for me to realize that most people in Ravenshire were power hungry bigots like his parents and as beautiful as Ravenshire must be, people like that were enough to ruin a place for anyone. Even someone who loved nature and animals as much as Raphael did. Maybe, if the people hadn't been so horrible to him, he would have thrived there and loved Ravenshire as much as he seemed to love this park. But then how would we have met?

I was so lost in my thoughts that I didn't see Pads return to my side and as I took my next step, I stumbled over him, losing my balance. I snapped my eyes shut as I braced myself for the pain but it never came.

Instead, warm, strong arms wrapped around me and pulled me against a firm chest, the fragrance of fresh grass and honey enveloping me as I tried to catch my breath, my heart galloping at an unsteady pace. It had been pretty tame this whole time, but obviously an adrenaline rush like that was hard to handle for it. In the next moment though, the warm tingle of Raph's magic washed through me and my heart slowly went back to its much calmer state of being.

"I think you just..." Raph started to say and I craned my neck to look up at him, noticing the twinkle of mischief in his eyes and knowing he was about to say something that would make me roll my eyes. Still, I waited for him to speak, going so far as to raise a brow at him to urge him on.

He bit his lip, a smile flitting to his lips, loose strands of blond hair fluttering in the light breeze as he spoke. "I think you just...fell for me."

I watched him for a moment, wondering if he'd somehow forgotten our confessions from like an hour ago, but he just winked at me, the smile on his face widening. I rolled my eyes at him even as I chuckled because of how adorably dorky he was.

"Put me down, you big doofus." My voice couldn't have been more full of affection and he grinned as he steadied me, still keeping his arm wrapped around my waist as if he was reluctant to let go.

Raphael chuckled softly at my expression before leaning forward and pressing a sweet kiss on my cheeks that almost had me melting into goo in his arms. Warm breath tickled my ear as he moved closer, whispering right against my lobe, "Don't worry, Jai. I promise I'll always catch you."

My face warmed as he pulled away and I couldn't *not* hook my arm around his neck and pull him closer. I claimed his lips with mine and hoped that he could feel it on my lips, the amount of love I felt for him in such a short time. He was my other half though, there was no doubt about that. We belonged with each other.

Raphael

As we walked through the park, I couldn't stop thinking about how much things had changed in the last eighteen hours. My mother's call last night had left me feeling gutted and as useless as I'd felt when I'd first moved here. I'd even had a moment where I'd wondered if Jai would give up on me too, once my powers were no longer useful to him, once he was completely healed. I knew he was nothing like my parents and I knew he was my semnyar and would never do that to me. And yet my mind had tried to tell me that he only cared about my magic, just like my family and everyone else.

But then I'd woken up with his mouth on me and he'd made me feel so good, not just with the best blowjob of my life but with his confession. He'd told me he loved me. As if he'd known exactly what I needed to hear, he'd told me that he would love me even if I lost all my magic. The moment he'd said those words, I'd realized how stupid I'd been to put him in the same box as I had my mother. Jai was warm and full of love and the complete opposite of my mother. I believed him when he said he'd love me without magic but I'd forever be grateful for it because my magic gave me the power to keep the pain away from my semnyar and that's all I'd ever want.

I looked down at where Jai walked by my side and as if feeling me watching him, he looked up with a smile, brow quirked in question. I didn't want to tell him what I'd been thinking, what my mind had almost made me believe, how unfair I'd been to him. So I let my goofy side take over, something I only did with him because it made him smile and his smile was the most beautiful thing to me in the whole world.

I gazed into his soft, muddy brown eyes for a moment before letting out a soft gasp. As I expected, Jai's brows furrowed in confusion as he kept his gaze locked with mine. "Angel?"

Damn, I loved it when he called me that. The look of awe I gave him wasn't even faked and I watched the furrow between his eyes deepen as he stopped walking and turned towards me fully. "Raph? What is it?"

"It's your eyes, Jai," I murmured and even I could hear the thick layer of awe in my voice.

His head jerked back and he bit his lower lip. "What about my eyes?" He asked, voice slightly too defensive for my taste.

Did he seriously think I was going to say something bad about him?

I took his face between my palms, hoping my expression looked as serious as I was trying to make it look. "Why...Jai...They're the most mesmerizing, most beautiful eyes I've ever seen."

Jai's mouth opened slightly as if he wanted to say something before he closed it and I felt his cheeks warm up under my palms as he tried to pull away.

I smiled widely at him before leaning forward and kissing both his cheeks. When I finally let go, he slapped my arm lightly, ducking his head as he grabbed onto my arm. "You're such a flirt," he mumbled, his usually firm voice sounding shy as he avoided looking up at me.

I wrapped my arm around him, pulling him into my side as I shrugged. "Just telling it as I see it. You'll have to deal with this for your whole life, you know. Are you up for that?" The question was meant as a joke but I still held my breath as I waited for him to answer.

"Am I up for spending my life with a man who makes me feel whole and not just that, but beautiful? Who is happy to slow down so he could stay by my side and who shows me his love for me in everything he does? I'd be a lunatic if I even thought about giving up on something like that. Not to mention, I don't think I could survive it, and that has nothing to do with what your magic can do for my body. My heart, my soul wouldn't be able to take that, got it?" Jai's eyes were full of fire as he demanded an answer and I nodded, licking my suddenly dry lips. Damn, I loved it when he was firm and full of fire like he was right now.

His eyes tracked my tongue as it went and then he was leaning up on his toes to taste my lips himself. I pulled him closer to me, my arms wrapping tightly around him as his fingers tightened in my hair and pulled me to him.

As our tongues tangled together, my palms ran down his back, feeling every ridge of his spine and ribs underneath as I reached his cute little butt. I squeezed his cheeks, making him moan into my mouth. Before he could realize what I was doing, I leaned down, pressing my palms to the back of his thighs and hitching them up. Instinctively, Jai followed my movement, wrapping his legs securely around my waist as I pressed his back against the trunk of a tree nearby.

As I plunged my tongue back into his mouth, moaning at the sweet taste of him, I remembered this part of the semnyar bond. Now that we'd finally delved into the physical side of our relationship, keeping away from touching Jai was going to be almost impossible for a while. It was one of the reasons why I'd wanted to go slow, because I knew once we started making love there would be no going back. But now that Jai had told me he loved me, nothing was going to stop me from making him mine in every sense of the word.

My hips thrusted against him of their own accord, my dick rubbing against his pert ass and making me groan. Pulling away from his mouth, I leaned back a little so I could unbutton Jai's jeans. His hand shot out to stop me just as I was pulling the zipper and I looked up at him, desire written all over my face.

He was a picture of lust, with his hair in a disarray and his dark pink lips swollen from all the kissing. "Someone could walk by!"

I looked around before spotting Neya seated on a tree branch a few yards away, her back to us. "Hey, Neya. Could you maybe let me know if someone is close?"

I felt her agreement—and glee, for some reason—through the bond and nodded. "Thanks."

"Neya says she'll keep a watch."

"You can talk to her?"

"Do you really want to talk about this right now?" I asked, thrusting my hips to emphasize my point.

Jai shook his head and I leaned forward to nibble a bit on his plump lower lip before pulling back and resuming what I'd been doing.

Once I had both our cocks out, I took them in my palm, my mouth watering at the sight of my semnyar's thick cock. His wasn't as long as mine, but it was uncut and thicker. I couldn't wait to get it into my mouth.

I kissed Jai again as I pumped us together, moaning into his mouth as he whimpered quietly. He didn't seem to make much noise while I worked, just quiet, barely there whimpers as I jacked our lengths together.

I rested my forehead against his, our breaths coming out in short pants that were almost in sync. "Shit!" I hissed just before I came, my cum shooting out in a thick stream and hitting Jai right in the chin. His head craned back as he bit his lip and then his cum was joining mine on his t-shirt and my hand. I rested my forehead on his chin as I tried to catch my breath, and my magic washed over him almost instinctively as I realized he was getting out of breath.

Once he'd calmed down, I pulled back and looked at him to find him smirking at me. "Did you seriously just magic me through my dick?"

I looked down at where I was still holding our dicks together and laughed when I realized it was the only place I was touching him skin to skin.

I shook my head as I pulled my hand away and licked our shared cum off my fingers. It wasn't like I had tissue paper here, right?

When I looked up, Jai was watching me with hooded eyes and I grinned when his dick jerked. I gave him a show, licking each and every finger slowly and thoroughly as he groaned, tucking himself back inside.

"Stop teasing me."

I laughed as I wrapped my—now clean—palms around his hips and helped him stand up. The cum on his t-shirt had almost dried, so I zipped his jacket close to hide the stain, smiling when he looked down to see what I was doing.

"Fuck, that was my favorite t-shirt. It will wash off, right?"

I chuckled, feeling warm and sated and happier than I ever had. "Yes, it'll wash off. How about we go home, put it in the washer and then cuddle and maybe watch a movie for a while?"

Jai looked up at me, eyes bright as he linked his fingers with mine. "Sounds perfect."

EIGHTEEN

Jai

The next two months passed by in a haze of love and happiness. We did a lot more things from my "wishlist." We made a weekend trip to an amusement park where I experienced my very first roller coaster ride, went on the zip line and even dared to enter the Haunted House. I discovered that my fear of creepy things had absolutely nothing to do with my weak heart. At home, I even managed a *run* around the cul-de-sacs. I ran the same distance I hadn't even been able to walk the first time we met.

Every moment I spent with Raphael was beautiful and I still found it hard to believe that I would get to do it for a long, long time.

My parents were pleasantly surprised at the sudden, massive improvements in my health and at Raphael's steady presence in my life. My mom absolutely adored him and I loved watching him revel in her motherly love—even though technically he was far older than her, a fact that always made me chuckle. The love she gave him was something he should've received from his own bitch of a mother, but I was glad he was getting my mom's love. My mom was the best mother who ever mothered. She'd realized the moment I introduced them that he needed some gentle loving and that's what she gave him.

We were headed over to my parents' for the monthly dinner, something Raph was also required to attend, as per my mom's orders. Like every time we went, Raphael was running around in his room, trying to pick an outfit while I watched from the doorway. It was bittersweet, because on one hand he looked adorable as he ran around the room but on the other hand the fact that he felt like he had to be at his best or my mom would suddenly stop loving him broke my heart. I'd tried to tell him so many times that nothing would stop my mom from doting on him and he'd nod and say he understood every time and then go back to panicking like this. I didn't know what to do, what to tell him to convince him that my mother loved him.

"Why don't you wear your white button down and the dark blue denims? You look gorgeous in those," I said as I walked into the room. Well, he looked gorgeous in everything but I needed him to get ready or we'd be late.

"You think so?" He asked, running his hand through his hair.

"I know so."

He nodded and started changing while I stood there and watched him because I could. Not my fault he was so fucking gorgeous

Once he was dressed, I waved him over. "Come here, give me a hug."

He was in my arms in a second, holding on tight. The way he clung to me told me he'd needed the hug. I held him tight, my face pressed against his pec as I kissed the place I could feel his heart beating against. "I'm right here with you, okay?

My family loves you and they won't care if you're ten minutes late or an hour or if you show up in your sleep clothes. They already consider you a part of the family and so do I."

Raph nodded against the top of my head and I kissed his pec again, wishing I could do more. But all I could do was stay by his side and show him that not all families were the way his had been. I wanted him to see that he was now a part of a real family. One that was loving and caring and safe.

Raphael

We were thirty minutes late. I knew, in some part of me, that it wasn't a big deal, that Jai's mom wouldn't care, but I still couldn't *not* worry. I liked Jai's mom. Actually, I loved her. She was everything my mother had never been and the thought of disappointing her didn't sit well with me.

Jai knocked on the front door of his parents' place—apparently, he had returned his keys to his mom in an attempt to show her that he really meant to move out. It was a cute little house that was just a five minute drive from our places. A five minute drive and yet we were late. I chewed on my thumbnail in an effort to calm myself, but it only served to make Jai realize just how nervous I was.

"Calm down, Angel. I promise none of them give a shit if we're late." I nodded at Jai even though all I could hear in my mind was my mother's voice telling me that I could never do *anything* right and telling me how absolutely useless I was. I knew it was stupid to worry. I was more than a century old, for mother's sake. I shouldn't care what Jai's mom thought of me. I shouldn't *want* for her approval and love the way I did.

I shook off the familiar bitterness as the door opened and Joy grinned at us. His blue eyes brightened the moment he saw

Jai, lighting up from within. I loved Joy for that, for loving his brother so much. This was what a *real* family was, right? And now I was a part of it.

"Hey *bhai*, hey Raphael. Come on in, mom's made your favorite."

"Paneer Masala?" Jai asked eagerly before turning to me and explaining, "It's cubes of cottage cheese fried and then cooked in curry. You'll love it."

I smiled because I *would* love it. Neha Presley was one helluva cook and I loved everything she made.

Jai took my hand in his as if he knew I was losing it and squeezed. I shot him a grateful smile as I linked our fingers and walked into the open plan living room and kitchen. Jai's mom and dad were both in the kitchen, working around each other with an ease that spoke of years spent working side by side.

"Hey Ma!" Jai called a greeting and I almost chewed my lower lip off as I waited for her to speak.

Mrs. Presley, who insisted I call her Ma too, wiped her hands on a washcloth before walking around the counter and straight towards us with a smile.

I swallowed hard and almost choked on my spit when she pulled me into a tight hug, patting my back in a move that instantly calmed me. She had a warm, comforting aura and her hug squeezed the anxiety right out of me.

"Hey sweet boy. You okay?" She asked, her Indian accent still as thick as ever. She pulled back, a slight crease between her brows as she waited for me to answer.

"I'm fine, Ma." I smiled at her, a genuine smile now that I knew she didn't care about us being late. Now that I'd calmed down though, I realized how stupid I'd been. Jai's mom was nothing like the cold, hurtful Helena Woodward and I needed to remember that.

Neha Presley was sweet, gentle and caring and she considered me a part of her family. She'd never treat me the way my mother had, it just wasn't possible.

"I see how it is. Now that you have a prettier son, you're just going to forget about me, aren't you?" Jai joked, making Ma roll her eyes at her son.

"Of course not. How could I forget my miracle baby?" Jai's smile fell just for just a second at her words, but even if I hadn't seen that, I clearly felt the annoyance tinged with hurt through our quickly strengthening bond. What had made him react that way? I remembered a conversation months ago when he'd mentioned that his mom liked calling him her miracle. Did he not like that?

Jai hugged his mom, his smile firmly back in place when he pulled back. Ma looked Jai over for a minute and her smile widened. "Have you gained weight, *beta*?"

"A bit," Jai admitted with a small grin and my own smile widened proudly, not just because my semnyar was getting healthier each day but because of how much happier he looked than the man who had fallen to his knees in front of my house a few months ago. The reason for some of that happiness was me. That part was still kinda hard to believe.

As we ate Ma's food—the paneer masala as delicious as Jai had promised it to be, paired with butter rotis and salad—I marveled over how happy I felt with these people I'd met just a few short months ago, while a century and half with my own family had barely been tolerable. I knew the joy I felt with Jai was thanks to our bond, but I'd never expected to feel so close to his family.

There was so much laughter in this family, so much joy and finding my semnyar in Jai couldn't have been any more rewarding.

After dinner, the cleanup fell to me, Jai and Joy, but I made Jai sit on the counter while I washed and Joy dried. No way was I going to make my semnyar work.

Joy looked over his shoulder, turning his head this way and that to make sure his parents weren't in hearing distance. Once he was satisfied, he turned to look at me, a curious quirk to his brow that was so like Jai's it made me grin.

"What?" I asked, the laughter clear in my voice.

"I was wondering...can't you, like, magic them clean?" Joy asked and I chuckled. So like his elder brother.

"Unfortunately, no. That's not how it works. I have some inherent magic that lets me do small stuff like manipulate the air around us a bit. But my strength is nature and healing magic, so that's what I'm good at. Now, Cassian could probably burn every last bacteria off these dishes—as long as he didn't burn down the house first." Everyone in Ravenshire knew how deadly Cassian's fire was.

"Cassian?" Joy asked, his eyes widening and I cringed as I realized I'd just outed Cassian. Shit.

Joy turned to look at Jai, who sat at the counter, swinging his legs with an amused smile on his face while I wondered if Cassian Romanov would murder me. Surely, he wouldn't do that to his best friend's semnyar, right?

"*Your* Cassian?" Joy asked and I almost growled, my face scrunching up in a scowl. Jai was mine and I was his. *Not* Cassian.

The brothers chuckled at me as if my jealousy over my semnyar was *funny*. When I didn't answer Joy's question, Jai took over.

"Yeah, apparently. Cassian is a fire mage."

"Woah. So cool." As if remembering me, Joy patted my arm, a sweet smile on his face. "Not that your magic isn't just as awesome, of course." I couldn't blame him, though. Fire magic *was* cool.

Once the dishes were done, Joy headed up to his room after hugging his brother goodnight. Jai's parents were in the living room and I assumed that's where we were headed, but instead Jai took me out the back door. The backyard was small, but well-kept and I smiled when Jai led me to a two-person swing on the porch. It was comfy enough for the two of us and I wrapped my arm around my semnyar as he sank onto me, his head coming to rest on my shoulder.

By now, my magic was almost on auto mode as it seeped into him, working on his lungs and heart a bit by bit. He didn't get as tired anymore, so I'd started focusing more and more on the root of all his discomfort.

"You're doing it again, aren't you?" Jai asked, turning his head to look up at me with a smirk on his face.

Since I could never resist my gorgeous man, I leaned forward and gave his lips a peck, not wanting his parents to catch us making out but also unable to stay away.

"My magic is so attuned to you now that I don't even have to consciously think about it." I admitted, making him smile. He snuggled closer to me, his arm wrapping around my waist and I sighed in contentment. This was what I'd spent more than a century looking for. This peace, this quiet joy, this love.

"Jai, why don't you like it when your mom calls you a miracle?" I asked. The question had been at the back of my mind since it happened, but I hadn't wanted to say anything in front of his family. Jai stiffened in my arms before sighing loudly and melting into me.

"You noticed that, huh? It's not a big deal. Pretty stupid, actually."

I waited him out, knowing he would tell me if he wanted to.

"Well, my mom loves telling this story to everyone, but when I was a baby, my doctor told my parents that I wouldn't survive past six months of age. And now here I am, still alive, twenty-three years later. I think for Ma it's more of a 'I proved them wrong' thing, but every time she says it, all I can think is I will never have a full life, that though I survived past six months, I'm always gonna live in pain and even then I won't get a full life."

Before I could remind him that he *would* get to live a full life, a gasp behind us made me look back and my heart fell when I saw Jai's mom standing in the doorway, a palm covering her mouth and tears in her eyes. Shit.

"Fuck!" Jai muttered under his breath before scrambling out of my arms and rushing to his mom. Without a word, he pulled her into his arms, holding her to him and murmuring softly in her ear.

She pulled back after a moment, wiping her eyes with the back of her hand. "I'm sorry, I didn't mean to eavesdrop. I'm sorry, *beta*. I didn't realize how you felt about that."

Jai shrugged, giving her a sheepish smile as I wrapped my arms around him from behind. He sank into me instantly, as if he just couldn't support himself any longer. "I never told you, so it's not your fault, Ma."

Ma nodded, shook her head and then smiled brightly at us. "I made brownies. Would you like to eat some as dessert before you leave?"

I nodded instantly, making both of them laugh and I smiled to myself as I followed them into the house. Making them laugh and keeping them happy was all I ever wanted to do because for the first time in my life, I had a *real* family and I would do anything for them.

NINETEEN

Jai

The moment I closed the door behind me, Raph pulled me into his arms, his lips descending on mine with an intensity that made me wonder if tonight would be the night. The night my soulmate made love to me.

Raph's lips were soft against mine and I licked into them, moaning when he opened his mouth and granted me entry into his sweet mouth that tasted of brownies and him. My palms slid underneath his shirt, mapping over his back, his skin warm and familiar against mine.

I pulled away with a gasp when my lungs started burning from the lack of oxygen and opened my eyes. I hadn't even realized I'd closed them.

Raph's pupils were blown, his eyes dark with lust and I whimpered low in my throat as I met his gaze. Taking a deep breath, I voiced my question. "Will you make love to me, Raphael?"

Raph's eyes widened slightly before darkening further and then he was on me, kissing, licking, nipping at my lips and turning me into a mess.

"I'd love nothing more, my semnyar. Will you let me mark you?" He murmured against my neck, his warm breath blowing over my skin and making me shiver.

"M-mark me?" I asked, my voice breaking when he licked up the side of my neck, his slight stubble brushing against my skin. I wasn't sure what he meant by that, since he'd never mentioned it before.

Raph pulled back to meet my eyes and maybe to gauge my reaction as he spoke, "Yeah. It'll be a small mark that would connect you to me and make our bond stronger."

"So, will you...bite me?" I asked, not completely sure how I felt about that. I'd love to have his mark on me, but the pain...

Raph chuckled and shook his head and I sighed in relief as he spoke, "No. Only shifters and vampires do that. I'll just place my palm on your chest and my magic will do the rest."

"Oh."

"So?" Raph asked and I realized how nervous he was when he started chewing on his thumbnail. This was a big step for both of us, a permanent mark that would make me his forever. The thing was, I was already his in all the ways that mattered.

"Please mark me, Raph. Make me yours."

Raph's eyes widened and it looked like he was tearing up but I couldn't be sure because his lips were on mine again. This kiss was sweeter, but just as intense and I sighed into his mouth as I pressed my body to his.

After a few minutes of kissing, he pulled back, taking my hands in his as he met my eyes. "I want to take my time with you. Is that okay?"

I nodded, too overwhelmed to make my voice work.

Raphael led me to my bedroom, shooing Pads out of my room with a sweet smile and gentle nudges before closing the door after him.

I pulled Raph closer, not wanting even a bit of space between us, and buried my face in his neck, breathing in his familiar grass and honey scent. "I love you, Raphael Woodward. I can't wait to be yours forever."

"You're mine, Jai. And I'm yours. Nothing and no one can change that."

I smiled as I pulled back and looked up into his unique eyes, at the smile on his lips. "You know, we never talked about it before, but I'm vers. I can always bottom if you prefer to top, though."

Raphael's eyes darkened as they scanned me from head to toe and I shivered at the intensity of his gaze. "I'd love to have you inside me someday, Jai. Today, I want to claim you, but soon I want you to take me too because I'm yours however you want me."

I moaned softly at all the dirty images in my head and buried my face in his neck, breathing him in as I licked and kissed and nipped at his skin. Sure, I couldn't leave a permanent mark on him but that didn't mean I couldn't mark him.

When I pulled back, I smiled in satisfaction at the unmissable hickey at the base of his neck.

"Did you just mark me?" Raph asked, a wide smile on his face as he touched his neck and shuddered when his fingers touched the now sensitive skin.

I shrugged as I looked him over, my eyes snagging on his crotch. I stared at the huge bulge, licking my lips. I couldn't wait to get him inside me.

Raph pulled me closer, pecking my lips as his hands wrapped around my hoodie, a question in his eyes.

I raised my arms up for him and he smiled as he slid first my hoodie and then my t-shirt off me. His eyes roamed over my naked chest, making goosebumps pop all over my skin. The look in his eyes made me feel a hundred feet tall and like I was the most gorgeous man in the world.

I'd filled out a little in the past few months, but I was still a bit bony at my hips and you could still see my ribs and the knobs of my spine, but somehow Raphael made me believe that they didn't take away from my good looks. He'd spent many hours licking and tracing every rib, laving his tongue over the knobs of my spine until all I thought about when I saw them was him and what he'd done to me.

Raphael's fingers trailed over my skin, light as a feather. Somehow, the light touch felt like it was leaving burn tracks on my skin. I'd never felt like this before and even though it was my first everything, I knew the only reason it felt so good was because Raph was the one doing it.

My hands reached for the buttons of his shirt and he moved closer, giving me all the permission I needed. I unbuttoned his shirt slowly, savoring each new reveal of skin. His chest was smooth, with just the lightest brush of blond hair and his muscles were just enough to give my hands a lot of dips and creases to explore without him looking like a gym junkie. I loved his body. I loved his pretty pink nipples that pebbled over as soon as I uncovered them and I couldn't resist leaning over and sucking the left one into my mouth.

Raphael moaned softly, his hands tightening around my hips. I'd discovered a lot of things about him in the past few months, one of which was that he loved it when I played with his nipples. And so I did. I licked, sucked and nipped at those gorgeous pink nipples until he was pulling away, panting, his lips swollen from all the kissing and chewing on them.

"Enough. You're going to make me come." Raphael took a deep breath as I watched him, loving the dark flush that reached all the way to his chest. His hands reached for the button of my jeans and I nodded immediately. I was hard and aching and I needed him more than I'd ever needed him.

Raphael smiled at me, leaning forward to kiss my lips chastely before he unbuttoned my jeans and slid them down my legs. I grabbed his shoulder as he pulled them off, glad I'd removed my shoes and socks, though I couldn't for the life of me remember when. All I knew was I was now naked and Raph was watching me as if he wanted to devour me.

"Your turn," I said, my voice husky with lust as I grabbed the waistband of his pants. He spread his arms wide, as if saying *I'm all yours* and I grinned at him as I slid his pants off his legs. Of course, he was perfectly steady as I pulled them off and threw them somewhere behind me, to be found later.

I swallowed hard when my eyes fell on his huge cock. I'd taken it into my mouth more times than I could count, but would it fit in my ass? Would it hurt?

Warm palms cradled my face and tilted my head upwards. I hadn't even realized I'd been staring at his dick for so long.

Raphael met my eyes, a soft smile on his face. "We'll take it as slow as you need, okay?"

I nodded and Raph pulled me into his arms, his lips claiming mine, his tongue invading my mouth and exploring every crevice, every nook. I tangled my fingers into the soft strands of his hair, pulling him even closer as I moaned softly into his mouth.

I squeaked as he grabbed the backs of my thighs and hefted me up. I wrapped my legs tightly around his waist as he continued kissing me, holding on to me as he slowly walked backwards toward the bed. I pulled back, burying my face in his neck. I loved his scent and I loved the slightly salty, slightly grassy taste of him. It was so unique and so him.

I gasped as we fell on the bed, but Raph's arms around me kept me from getting jostled too much and I pulled back to look at him, shaking my head. "You okay?"

Raphael rolled his eyes but nodded and I was glad he knew me well enough to not joke about my weight. That would've been a mood killer.

I smiled at him as I kissed his lips softly before crawling down his body, licking and kissing and tasting all the gorgeous skin I could get my lips on. As I was playing with his cute little belly button, I was flipped onto my back and Raph hovered over me, his eyes dark and hooded. "Enough. My turn." His voice was hoarse and breathy all at the same time and I gasped as his mouth latched onto my nipple. Fuck, it was payback time.

"Damn, you taste so good." Raph moaned against my nipple and I blushed. I could hear nothing but honesty and a whole lot of lust in his voice and it just made me feel even more flustered.

I bit my lip as he nipped at the skin below my nipple, my body arching upwards without thought. "You like that, don't you?" Raphael asked and I nodded, having already lost my power of speech.

Raphael, who'd already explored every inch of my skin more times that I could count, went straight for the prize, swallowing my dick in one swoop and making me jerk as I tried not to force myself into his mouth. His hands spread across my ass and he pumped my dick, the wet warmth of his mouth making it impossible for me to not want to delve deeper.

When my orgasm started building up, I found my voice enough to gasp out, "Stop. I want...I want to come with you inside me."

Raphael pulled away, drool trailing down his chin as he licked his lips and I bit back a moan at how absolutely sinful he looked. My sinful angel.

Raphael winked at me before grabbing my ankles and directing me to fold my legs. I spread them wide as I pulled my knees as close to my body as I could. Flexibility wasn't my strong suit but Raph didn't seem to mind, so I wouldn't either.

Raphael crawled back a little before leaning forward and licking my hole with the flat of his tongue and making me shiver. My palms tightened around my legs as he traced the puckered skin of my hole with his tongue, licking and nipping until I was loose enough for him to delve his tongue deeper.

I didn't know how long he played with my hole, but suddenly he had one lubed finger into me, then two and when he finally inserted the third finger, I knew I wouldn't last long.

"I'm ready, Angel. Take me, please. Make me yours." He looked up, pupils blown wide as he nodded and sat up. He wrapped his lube coated fingers around his leaking dick, the head purple with need and I opened my mouth to protest but he beat me to it.

"Don't worry, baby. My magic keeps me and you healthy, always. We don't need condoms."

My cheeks warmed even more as I thought about Raphael spilling inside me, marking me as his from the inside. Oh gods. And, I would get to do the same to him soon. I swallowed hard as I nodded, my throat clicking audibly.

Raph positioned the head of his cock against my hole, pressing forward ever so slowly and I threw my head back at the way his dick stretched my hole. I pushed out and the head popped inside, making me bite my lip at how good and right it felt.

Raph didn't push further. Instead, he covered my body with his, taking my face between his palms and pressing his lips to mine. He kissed me softly, reverently as if I was the most precious thing in his world. As we kissed he slid into me inch by inch until his body was flush against mine and there wasn't an inch of space between us. He stayed like that for a moment, waiting for me to get used to the delicious fullness of him, before he started moving.

"One day, I'll take you hard and fast. Pound into you until you're screaming my name," Raph rasped out, his voice a hoarse whisper. "But today, I want to take it slow. I want to savor every moment. Is that okay?"

"Yes!" I couldn't help but imagine the scenario he spoke of and I shuddered as he slid almost all the way out of me before sliding in just as slowly, pressing against my prostate and making me gasp. It felt so good. It was as if for the first time in my life, I was complete. I was one with the other half of my soul, my semnyar and nothing had felt better.

Raphael kept up the steady pace, nipping at my lips, my chin, any skin he could get his mouth on. I felt my orgasm starting to build up again and my palms tightened on his shoulders. I squeezed my eyes shut, my body shaking as my orgasm rocked into me and I couldn't stop myself from moaning long and loud as it barreled through me. I was faintly aware of Raphael calling out my name before I felt his warmth spill inside me, his body shaking over mine as his palm came to rest on my chest, right over my heart.

The sudden warmth against my chest pulled me out of my post-orgasm haze a little. At first, I thought Raph was using his magic on me and I was about to ask him what the hurry was when I realized it felt different.

I gasped when Raph pulled his hand away and I got a look at my chest. A green, five petal flower had appeared on my skin, right over my heart. "Is that...?"

"Our mating mark," Raphael said, his voice just as full of awe and I looked up at him, my eyes widening when I realized he had the same mark over his heart.

I traced the flower lightly with my fingertip as tears of joy gathered in my eyes. "You have one too."

He looked down at himself before giving a surprised chuckle. When his eyes met mine, they glittered with unshed tears too. "I didn't know I would get one too."

"Why the green flower?"

Raphael shrugged, a wide smile on his face. "I've seen that flower in Ravenshire a time or two. It's called Greenwish and supposedly, finding it grants you good luck or fulfills a wish."

I smiled at him, pulling him into a hug even as my cum squelched between us and I remembered he was still inside me. "The day I fell in front of your place *was* the luckiest day of my life."

"Mine too. I'd been wishing I could find someone who'd love me for me, you know? And fate sent you." He ran his fingers across my back as he spoke and I soaked in his warmth, grateful to fate for bringing us together.

After a minute, Raph pulled back and pecked my nose before slowly pulling away, wincing when the almost dried cum pulled at his skin.

"I'll clean us up." He hopped off the bed and I sighed, stretching out the sore muscles, a wide smile on my face. I traced my tattoo with my fingertip and I could swear I felt Raph's joy through our bond.

Once he'd cleaned both of us up, we pulled on our underwear and opened the bedroom door to let our companions in. Like he did every night, Raph held me in his arms, with Padfoot splayed out on my other side and Neya curled over Raph's neck. I closed my eyes, basking in the feel of his arms around me and my baby boy behind me, keeping me safe. Before I knew it, I was asleep.

Raphael

I ran my fingers through Jai's hair, marveling over the fact that he was mine. This beautiful, smart human was mine. How did I ever get so lucky?

My eyes flitted towards the mark over his heart, a wave of joy and love washing over me. He was mine, for now and ever. Damn, I was the luckiest man in the world.

"Angel..." Jai murmured. I looked up at his face, expecting him to be watching me, but he was still asleep. His hand tightened around me almost reflexively. Was he dreaming about me?

I watched him, not at all creepily, as he slept. His eyelids fluttered every few minutes as he mumbled something incomprehensible in his sleep. He looked so adorable and I wanted to watch him sleep all night long.

I leaned forward slowly, not wanting to dislodge Neya from where she slept wrapped around my neck. I pressed a kiss on top of Jai's head and snuggled closer, letting my eyes fall shut. I breathed in his chocolate scent mixed with the salty scents of sex and sweat. The mix of scents just made him even more irresistible and I squeezed him tighter as I finally let sleep claim me.

***

The next morning, I woke up in bed with only Neya for company, but I could hear music coming from the living area, so I knew Jai was around. I cleaned up quickly and brushed my teeth before heading towards the living room. I stopped short in the doorway, grinning at the sight that greeted me.

Jai stood in the kitchen, dressed in just an apron and his underwear and he was dancing to the song playing on the radio while holding both of Padfoot's front paws in his hands. I bit back a chuckle at the duo, wondering if this was a daily occurrence and how the hell had I never seen this before if it was?

Jai laughed in delight as he moved, making me smile wider. I was just about to go and join him when his eyes met mine and then widened visibly as he dropped Padfoot's paws, looking flustered and adorable.

I bit my lip to keep from laughing but a small chuckle slipped past as I walked over to my semnyar. I extended a hand, palm up towards him and he looked at me curiously as if he had no clue what I was about to ask.

"May I have the next dance?"

Jai shook his head at me but took my hand and I pulled him flush against me, rocking gently even though the song he'd been dancing to was a fast-paced party song. I curled my arm tightly around his waist and used my free hand to trail my fingers down his cheek. I smiled when his eyes fluttered shut and he arched his neck back to give me better access. I trailed my fingers all the way to his mark. I couldn't get enough of seeing it, of touching it and cherishing it.

I retraced my steps and tangled my fingers in his hair, pulling him closer so I could kiss him. He tasted of toothpaste and mint and that underlying sweetness that was just him. I didn't delve deeper, just played with his soft lips, tasting them, memorizing them.

Jai jerked back after a few minutes of kissing and his eyes widened. "The eggs!"

He ran back to the counter and I watched his boxer clad butt as he raced around dumping the now burnt scrambled eggs. It sucked that his work had gone to waste, but frankly I didn't care if we just ate toasts and drank tea for breakfast. As long as we were together to do it, I'd be fine.

TWENTY

Jai

I ran my fingers through Raph's silky blond hair, smiling at the quiet contentment on his face as he lay with his head in my lap. His backyard had become a special place for the two of us and our furry companions. It was our very own slice of heaven and I loved spending late afternoons here, just lazing around and talking about anything and everything that came to mind.

We talked about our childhoods and Raph's tales of times when phones and televisions didn't exist fascinated me to no end. He'd spent almost all his life in Ravenshire, only coming to the mainland every once in a while. He'd told me how he'd stopped coming here once he'd realized he didn't have magic like his parents and was of no use at the hospitals.

I still couldn't believe how stupid his parents were to give up on someone like him. Someone so warm, so free with his love, so giving...how could they not love him? I'd only known him for a few short months and mates or not, I couldn't imagine not loving him anymore, no matter what he did. If he told me tomorrow that he couldn't heal me anymore, I wouldn't even care as long as I got to keep him. Nothing would make me give up on him and I wish his parents had been the same.

"Hey, Raph?" I asked, needing to distract myself lest I end up getting my blood pressure high. The thought of his parents always made me fume.

"Yeah?" He asked, peeking one of his gorgeous eyes open to look at me.

"What's your biggest fear?"

He hummed as he thought about it, just like I'd known he would. That was another thing about him that I loved. He always took my questions seriously, whether I was asking what he wanted for dinner that night or a question like the one I'd just asked.

He opened his eyes then, a soft smile on his face. "You."

I jerked under him, my brows shooting up as I tried to figure out what he meant. "Me?"

"You have so much power over me, baby, so much more than you realize. I'm scared that one day you'll look in the mirror and see yourself as I see you. And I'm scared you'll realize just how amazing you are and that you deserve so much better than me..." He took a deep, shuddering breath as his voice broke and I wanted to interrupt as much as I wanted to let him speak. "I'm terrified you'll leave me."

I took a deep breath, thinking over what I wanted to say before I spoke, placing my palm against his cheek, because I needed to touch him at that moment. "I'm not like your parents, Angel." He flinched in my arms, telling me I'd been right. This was because of his gods-awful parents. Not only did they not deserve him, they were bastards for making Raph think that he deserved less or was less because of their own inability to love.

"I'm not like your asshole parents. I'm your soulmate, your semnyar and you are my other half. You are the one I love. You are the one I would move heaven and earth for. Not your magic. Not even your looks, Angel. Your soul speaks to mine and that's the part of you I love the most. I love how sweet you are, I love your goofiness, I love how caring you are. I love how you treat tiny little furry animals and humans with the same amount of care and respect. I love you for all of those things and I cannot even imagine a day where I'd want to leave you. So you need to get that fear right out of your head, okay? I'm not leaving you, not even if you want me too. You're stuck with me."

Raphael didn't say anything. Instead, he flipped onto his side and buried his face in my stomach. I rubbed his back as he sniffled into my shirt and I promised myself that if I ever came across his parents, I'd tell them exactly what I thought of them.

Raphael

It took me a few minutes to gather myself as Jai's words kept ringing in my ears. I smiled against his shirt as I finally let the words settle into my heart, knowing Jai would keep his promise because that's the kind of man he was. It didn't hurt that I could feel his sincerity through our bond. He'd meant every word he'd said and that meant more to me than anything.

I could feel him starting to fidget and I realized his legs must have started hurting from how long I'd splayed myself across them. I cursed silently before hopping to my feet and offering him my hand.

Jai grabbed my hand as he pulled himself up with a wince, dusting the back of his pants as he glared at me. "You're way too sprightly for an old man."

I grinned at him, dancing on my toes as I sent some healing magic to him through our joined hands. I was glad he didn't want to talk more about my impromptu breakdown. I'd rather just forget it—except for what Jai had said, of course.

I loved it when Jai teased me about my age because it reminded me that he accepted all of me, that he wasn't turned off by the fact that I was more than a century older than him. He'd taken it all in stride and I loved him for that. He'd been fascinated with the stories from my early years and now I wished I'd gone out more back then, if only so I had more stories to tell him now. But how could I have known in the 1880s that there would be a time when I could not just freely be with a man but one where I'd also find my semnyar in the most beautiful, most inquisitive man who ever existed?

"Is that so?" I asked with a cheeky grin, letting some more of my magic flow into him. "Let me show you just how sprightly I can be."

Once I was sure I'd taken away all of his discomfort, I pressed a kiss to his knuckles before dropping his hand. I headed towards the oak tree in the corner of the backyard and hopped up, climbing onto the lowest branch.

I watched as Jai walked closer to the tree and I grinned as an idea popped into my head. Carefully, I slid off the branch, hooking my knees around it so I hung upside down, my face inches from Jai's as my hair blew into his face with the breeze. He sputtered, pushing the hair away from his face. Damn, that hadn't been part of the plan.

"What are you doing?" Jai demanded, laughter seeping into his voice as he tried to fight off my unruly hair. I used a pinch of my magic to blow my hair the other way so I could look at him properly and stop assaulting him with my hair.

"Trying to kiss you?"

"You're gonna fall, Angel."

"Shut up and kiss me, Jai. I'm getting lightheaded here." I wasn't, not really, but I was starting to lose my grip on the branch and I really wanted that kiss before I fell.

Jai stepped forward and kissed me, and let me tell you, it was a lot more awkward than it is in the movies. The placement wasn't right and lips were where they shouldn't be, but it was my semnyar and me, so we worked it out.

Just as Jai pulled away with a chuckle, I lost my grip. Before I could face-plant—or break my neck—against the ground, I used my magic to control the air around me enough to flip me upright before I crashed.

It couldn't have taken more than a second and I wasn't sure how much Jai actually saw, but as soon as my feet touched the ground, he pulled me into his arms, hugging me tightly. "Holy fuck, you scared the shit out of me! How did you even survive a century and half after the kind of crazy shit you do?" Jai's voice was high-pitched and I could hear his panic which immediately made me wince with guilt. Shit. I hadn't meant to scare him.

"Hey, I'm okay, I swear. I'm a lot tougher than I look. And I've got magic on my side, remember?"

Jai grumbled against my chest but didn't pull away. On the contrary, his arms tightened around me further as he spoke. "You're not allowed to leave me either, you know that, right? You're not the only one who's afraid of being left behind."

"I know, baby. You're my other half. I belong with you just as much as you belong with me and I have no plans of ever leaving your side. I promise."

Jai sank against me and I held him close. He was my semnyar, the other half of my soul. I wouldn't survive without him now that I'd found him and I didn't want to try. I planned to stay with him, right by his side for the rest of our very long lives.

TWENTY-ONE

Raphael

I wriggled in my seat as I drove to the animal shelter. I had a surprise planned for Jai and I was looking forward to carrying it out today. Over the past few weeks, Jai had visited the shelter with me quite a few times. He was now best buds with Rebba and I was pretty sure he was planning on volunteering with me sooner or later.

I also knew that he really wanted to adopt a particular dog whose name rhymes with soup. I'd seen him watching the old dog with a longing look in his eyes way too many times. I didn't know what was holding him back from going ahead and adopting him, but my semnyar wanted Coop, so he would get Coop.

I'd already talked it over with Rebba and finished all the paperwork. Today after work, I would take Coop home with me. Home. I chuckled softly, realizing Jai had spent most of his time over the last week at my place, only going back to get more dog food when it ran out. Maybe I could also ask Jai to move in with me? Would he be okay with that or would he think it's too soon?

I felt like he'd be okay with that. Surely, he was feeling the same unease I felt now, even though we'd only been apart for less than half an hour? We weren't meant to stay apart and it was only logical we moved together, right? We'd been dating for around six months now. Plus, we'd already promised each other forever together, so moving in together would be the logical next step, wouldn't it?

I parked in the grocery store lot across the road, cataloging everything I needed to do at the shelter today in an attempt to put Jai at the back of my mind for the moment, impossible as it was. I liked working at the shelter and I didn't want to end up harming one of the little ones because I couldn't stop thinking about my sweet semnyar.

Getting out of my car, I swore as I dropped the keys. Thank mother I'd left Neya with Jai or she would have definitely teased me for my clumsiness. I bent forward to pick up the key and sensed someone behind me. Before I could turn to look who it was, pain flared up the base of my skull, making me lose my balance. I fell forward, my head slamming against the edge of the car. I slumped against it as blackness spread over my eyes and I started to lose consciousness. Everything had happened so fast and I had no idea what was going on, but my last thought before the darkness consumed me was that I was glad I'd left Neya with Jai. She'd keep him safe.

Jai

I frowned at the time on my phone. It was an hour past the time Raph was supposed to get home and all my texts had gone unanswered. Where was he? Was he okay? Why wasn't he replying?

Ugh, enough. I needed to do something or I'd go crazy with worry. Pulling up Rebba's number, I hit dial, hoping Raph was just stuck in some kind of animal emergency and not in trouble. There was no reason for me to think he was in trouble, except that I had a strange feeling in my chest, like something wasn't right.

"Hey Jai! S'sup?" Rebba's deep drawl rang through the phone and I crossed my fingers, took a deep breath and asked the question.

"Hey Rebba. Is Raphael still there?"

"What? No. Actually, he didn't show up at all. I thought he was taking a day off or something."

I slumped against Padfoot's warm, familiar body, trying to keep the panic at bay as I buried my fingers into his fur. He hadn't gone to work at all? Where could he be then? He wouldn't have gone somewhere else without telling me, right?

"He left for work at his usual time, Rebba. He's not home yet."

"Shit. Hold on, let me ask around. Maybe he just went off following some great adventure," Rebba joked, but I could hear the worry in her voice.

I heard footsteps, a few bangs and muffled words and what I was sure was a curse before I heard Rebba's voice again. "Jai..." She hesitated and I braced himself for whatever she was about to say, my heart thundering in my chest as I squeezed my eyes shut. The weird feeling in my chest only intensified as I waited for her to continue.

"Tell me," I said, voice small and heart heavy as dread filled my veins. Raph was okay. He had to be okay. I wouldn't survive otherwise.

"His car is where he parks every day. Door's open. His keys are lying by the door."

"Shit," I cursed, trying to keep the tears at bay because this wasn't the time. I needed to figure out what had happened.

"Do you want me to call the cops?" Rebba asked and my thoughts screeched to a halt. Could I? Did Raph even have a current ID? Was his name on the ID the same as his real name? What if it wasn't and I ended up outing him? Or what if he didn't exist in the system at all? But he must've needed some kind of identification to buy this house, right? Ugh.

"No, not yet. It could be an awful prank by one of his friends for all I know," I lied, hating myself for lying to her but knowing I couldn't tell her the real reason either.

"What friends?" her voice was full of disbelief and I cringed. Of course she knew Raph didn't have many friends.

"Awful ones, obviously. Let me ask around and I'll let you know. Could you do me a favor and take the car home with you or something?"

"No worries, I'll take care of it. Just let me know once you find him, 'kay? And Jai?"

"Yeah?" I asked, my voice thick with unshed tears.

"I know he's your semnyar and all of that, so don't hesitate to ask for help, okay?"

Rebba knew? Was she a supernatural too, then? The curious part of me didn't care about it right now, because all my mind power was focused on worrying about Raph. I hoped he was okay.

"Take care, Jai." The call clicked shut and I dropped the phone on the couch, staring at nothing as I tried to process. Raph was gone. There was no way he'd left willingly. Even if the open car door and keys hadn't been there as evidence, I would've known something had gone wrong. I could feel it down to my bones. Something was wrong with my semnyar and I needed to find him. Now.

Raph had promised me yesterday that he would never leave me and I knew he intended to keep his promise. Which meant someone had taken him. But why? What could they possibly want him for?

Could it be his parents? Since he'd repeatedly declined to go back to Ravenshire, had his parents decided to take him there against his will?

The panic I'd been trying to keep at bay raced back with a vengeance and I gasped as I tried to breath, my heart picking up a mad, galloping pace as my vision wavered, getting blurrier every second.

I snapped my eyes shut and tried to take a breath, counting backwards from twenty in Hindi in an attempt to get my mind to focus on something else. It was slow going and by the time I said "Ek," my voice was much steadier and my heart had returned to it's slightly faster than normal pace.

What was I supposed to do now? How would I even start looking for Raph? And what if he was at Ravenshire? I had no clue how to get there and no idea if a measly human could even get in. Raph had talked about portals but he'd never really told me where they were.

"Shit!" I scampered to my phone as I realized that I did have an in. I had a best friend who lived somewhere on that island and who cared about me enough that I knew he would do everything in his powers to help me, recluse or not.

I pulled up Cassian's number and my thumb froze over the call button. Neither of us was a fan of calling, but right now I didn't think I had enough wherewithal to text him everything. I just hoped he'd pick up.

He answered on the first ring, his voice rich with a deep timbre. "Jai? You okay?" How he knew something was wrong was beyond me. Or maybe it was the fact that I was calling him that clued him in.

"Cassian…" I breathed out, my voice breaking as I fought to keep myself from breaking down completely. I had to be strong right now because Raph needed me.

"What's wrong, Jai?"

"Raph's missing. He went to work and his co-worker found his car door lying open and his keys on the ground. Someone took him, Cass. He'd never leave willingly."

"He's your semnyar, right?" Cass asked, his deep voice softening slightly.

"Yes."

"Then he was taken. What are you going to do? What can I help with?"

I smiled despite the situation. I'd known Cass would help me. He always did. "I don't know. I don't know if I should call the cops because I don't know if he's even got a current ID or what. I was wondering if his parents took him."

"His parents?"

"They're assholes. They verbally abused him all his life. They've been trying to get him to come back to Ravenshire ever since they found out he has magic. Could they have taken him back to Ravenshire?"

"Assholes sounds about right. It's possible, though I can't imagine any sane mage trying to separate one from his semnyar. I'll ask April to look around, though. Send me a picture of your man so I can show it to her. Send your address too. If I don't find him here, I'll come over to help you find him."

"You will?" My eyes widened at his offer. He'd always been adamant about not meeting and Raph had said he was a recluse even in Ravenshire. Yet, he was willing to come over? For me?

"Of course I will, Jai. You're my closest friend. There's no way I'm letting you deal with this alone."

"Thank you."

"Stay strong, Jai. I'll be there early tomorrow morning, with Raph if he's here and without him if he's not. Try to get some sleep and look for his familiar. He may have left her with you. She's connected to him, so even if she can't speak, she can answer your yes or no questions."

I was on my feet before he finished speaking and once he'd ended the call, I was looking around the room, trying to find the sweet, pesky squirrel.

"Neya? If you're here, please help me." There was a soft clicking sound and then a tug at my sleep pants. I looked down to see Neya trying to climb up the loose cloth of my pants. I offered my hand and Neya immediately climbed up, curling her tail around my wrist.

I held my palm up so we were eye to eye and asked, "Can you answer a few questions for me?"

Neya nodded emphatically and I was reminded of the mouse from Stuart Little as I smiled at her. "Is Raphael okay?"

She nodded immediately and I sighed in relief. "Did someone take him against his will?"

She nodded again and I bit my lip, hoping the answer to my next question wouldn't be yes for Raph's sake. But I was also hoping it would be yes for my own sake. "Did his parents or someone from his family take him?"

Neya shook her head and I didn't know whether I should be relieved or not. The only idea I'd had was a dead end. Where could Raph be?

"Is he coming back, Neya?" I asked, my voice barely above a whisper.

Neya nodded, her tiny eyes solemn and wiser than I'd expected them to be. She clambered up my arm and curled herself around my neck. I gasped softly when I felt the familiar warmth of Raph's magic. It wasn't seeping into me like it usually did, but instead surrounding me. As if Raph was hugging me through Neya.

"Come back home soon, my Angel. We're waiting for you."

TWENTY-TWO

Raphael

I came to with a blinding headache and a deep pain in my chest that I knew without a doubt came from my semnyar. Why was he hurting? What was wrong with him?

It took me a long few minutes to remember what had happened and realize that the pain Jai was in was because of me. Because I wasn't there with him. I'd been planning on surprising Jai tonight...and then someone had hit me in the back of my head when I got out of the car this morning.

I kept my eyes closed as I took stock of myself. My hands were tied behind my back in a loose enough hold that I'd be able to get out easily when the time came and other than that, I wasn't bound in any other way. Interesting. It was as if they weren't even trying to keep me here. Why was I here anyway? And where was *here*?

Now that I was awake, my magic was quick to dispel the pulsing headache. I was pretty sure I'd have gotten a concussion if I didn't have my magic. They'd gotten me good.

Once I knew my body was back to a hundred percent, I opened my eyes, immediately coming face to face with a strangely familiar face. I squinted as I tried to figure out where I'd seen him. The man seemed to be in his early forties, with a few strands of gray in his black hair. His almond shaped eyes watched me, his gaze sharp but not cold.

"Hello, Mr. Woodward. I apologize for the circumstances we're meeting under. My name's William Hawthorne."

I quirked a brow at him as he spoke. Somehow, I had a feeling his intentions weren't to hurt me. I just hoped I wasn't wrong because I wasn't the only one at risk if something happened to me. I had a semnyar and a semlee to worry about too. And that meant I'd only hang around long enough to figure out an escape route.

"I don't think kidnappers usually introduce themselves."

As I ran his name over in my mind, I remembered where I'd seen him. On the TV one night when Jai had been watching the news. He was the CEO of some big-shot info-tech company. I remembered the headline his face had accompanied and gasped as I realized why I was here.

"You want me to heal your daughter," I murmured and he nodded. He ran his fingers through his hair, showing me he was actually nervous under that calm façade. My flight instinct had already disappeared though, because now that I'd remembered who he was, I also remembered the picture of the little girl they'd shown. She had cancer, if I remembered correctly.

"Yes. I'm sorry for bringing you here like this, but my daughter needs your help. Please help her, Mr.Woodward."

"Call me Raphael. And how did you find me?"

He sighed, the sound filled with such a bone deep exhaustion that it made me want to pull him into a hug and lend him some of my magic despite the fact that he'd kidnapped me. Damn those healer's instincts.

"I was at the hospital for Camille's chemo appointment and some of the doctors were talking about you. It sounded a bit crazy to me, honestly, but I'm willing to try anything if it means my daughter can get to live a full life."

"Why didn't you just come up to me and ask me like a normal person? Did you really think I would say no to helping a little girl?"

William shook his head. "I didn't have time. The doctor said she only had a few more days, a week at most before her conditions deteriorated. I'd waited too long for the chemo and the medicines to work. I couldn't risk you saying no or giving me a fucking date or something."

"I'll help you. But I need to call someone first. My partner would be worried about me."

"Jai Presley, right?"

I bristled at the fact that he knew my semnyar's name. I couldn't help but feel that it was a veiled threat. He knew where my semnyar was and he wouldn't hesitate to use him for his benefit.

I narrowed my eyes at him as I straightened, crossing my arms over my chest. I'd unbound my arms as we talked and his eyes widened just the tiniest bit as he realized that.

"If you even touch my boyfriend, you will regret it, do you understand? You may not believe in magic, but you'd do well to remember this: we're connected. If anything happens to him, I won't be able to heal your girl."

He nodded swiftly as he spoke, "I just meant to say I'll have one of my people call him and let him know you're okay while you see my daughter." I didn't like that at all. I wanted to talk to Jai myself, to assure him that I was okay. But the thought of the little girl in pain kept me from arguing. Maybe they'd let me call him later?

"You better do that."

With a nod, he waved at someone and a woman in high heels and a professional, navy suit pants walked over. He told her to call Jai and let him know I was okay and would be *returned* as soon as I'd finished helping them.

William then gestured towards the door and it was only then that I realized we were in a bedroom—a guest room, maybe. William led me down a hallway and as I looked around, I realized he was rich. Very rich. No wonder he expected me to do his bidding. The man was used to it.

"You'll be compensated for your time and...powers, of course," William said as he stopped in front of a closed door. A fancy name plate etched with animal cartoons marked the room as *Camille's* and I nodded as he opened the door. I didn't exactly need the money, but now that I had my semnyar, I was looking forward to spoiling him for the rest of our very long lives, so I wouldn't say no to it either. It wasn't like the man couldn't spare it.

I smiled when my eyes fell on the tiny little thing sleeping in the middle of the bed. She'd lost her hair to chemo, which made her look even younger somehow. She was hooked to a mask and IV and a dozen other devices that I had no clue about. I walked closer to her and took a deep breath before turning towards her father.

"How old is she?"

"Eight," William whispered in a hoarse voice and I gave him a soft smile.

"I can't promise you anything, William. I only discovered my powers a few months ago and so far, I've only healed my partner. I'm not sure how long it will take or if she will ever be completely back to normal, but I'll try my best."

"That's all I can ask."

I nodded as I looked around the room. The walls were covered with posters of tennis players and tennis rackets of different sizes hung from hooks on one wall. Not to stereotype, but the room was surprisingly not-pink. "She likes tennis?"

I looked up to see William wipe away a stray tear as he cleared his throat. "Her mother played tennis. She died when Cam was three, but Cam has always wanted to be just like her. The worst part of being sick for her has been that she couldn't play anymore."

I squeezed his shoulder in support. The calm and collected CEO I'd met a few minutes ago was gone, and in his place stood a single father barely holding on as he watched his daughter suffer. I couldn't imagine what he was going through, but I found myself forgiving him for the way he'd gotten me here. He was just a father trying to save his daughter. How could I begrudge him for that? "I'll need a chair and maybe something to eat? Magic needs a lot of energy and my body already spent a bit on healing myself."

William nodded and started walking backwards to the door. "I'll get you anything you need."

"William?" He stopped in the doorway and looked back at me. "I promise to do my best to make sure Camille gets to play tennis again."

William gave me a wobbly smile, nodded and then left the room.

I ran my finger down Camille's cheek, biting my lip at the pain she was in. I would help her. But first, I needed to make sure my semnyar was okay.

I closed my eyes and focused on our bond. I could feel his love for me, but it was hidden under a deep layer of unease. Did that mean he knew I was gone? How long had it been since I was taken? I should've asked William that, I realized as I looked for a clock around the room. There wasn't one.

I focused on my bond with Neya and told her everything that had happened and to keep an eye on Jai for me. She showed me a picture of the three of them in our backyard and I smiled, tucking away the memory in my mind for later.

When William returned, I asked him if Jai had been called yet, he told me his PA was doing just that and it took all my self-control to not go running to her so I could hear my semnyar's voice.

I took a seat in the chair William had brought and took Camille's hand, determined to heal the girl and make sure she could play again.

Jai

My phone started ringing as I walked across the length of the room once more. Padfoot had followed me around the first few times but now he sat on the couch following me with his eyes, a sad look on his face.

I couldn't stop worrying, despite Neya's reassurances. I knew she was much more intelligent than a common squirrel but it was still difficult to take her advice to heart, especially when it concerned the well-being of the man I loved.

I grabbed the phone off the coffee table and hit answer without checking who it was. "Hello?"

"Mr. Jai Presley?" A woman's voice spoke on the other end, calm and professional.

"Speaking," I said, slowing down as I wondered who was calling me.

"Mr. Presley, this call is to let you know that your partner, Mr. Woodward is in safe hands and he'll be returned to you as soon as he finishes his work for us."

"Work? What work? And where is he? Is he okay?"

"I'm sorry, I'm not at liberty to tell you that. I can assure you that he is well taken care of and will not be harmed."

"You can't kidnap my boyfriend and expect me to believe you won't hurt him," I snapped at her, frustrated at her non-answers. Where was my angel? Would they really not hurt him? And what work could they possibly want him to do?

"I'm sorry sir, but you'll have to believe me. Have a good evening!" The woman ended the call before I could speak and I dropped my phone on the couch as I resumed my pacing.

"Good evening, my ass," I muttered. "What the fuck could they want him for? What the fucking he—" I froze as I realized what anyone would want from Raph. The same thing his mother had wanted. His magic. Shit.

Could someone have kidnapped Raph to ask him to heal their loved one? But then, why not just ask him?

Ugh, this was turning more and more like the plot of a book. All I needed now was a mustache curling villain and we'd be good. Or was that only in movies?

I groaned at the wayward thoughts and looked up at the clock to check the time. It had been hours since Cassian's call, hours past bedtime, though I had no clue exactly how long I'd been pacing.

My eyes widened as I realized it was five in the morning already. Where had the night gone? And who the fuck called at five in the morning to tell people they'd kidnapped their boyfriend? What kind of alternate universe had I ended up in?

Before I could go down another rabbit hole, the doorbell rang, pulling me out of my thoughts. Was Cassian here?

I opened the door and looked up...and up...and up. Damn, the guy was tall. And huge. Even if the short red hair and the fiery yellow-orange eyes hadn't told me who he was, the eagle-owl on his shoulder would have. April. She was so much bigger than she looked in the pictures.

"Cassian!" I rushed him, wincing because he had way too many muscles and I'd just bodily slammed myself into them. I wrapped my arms around him, scrunching up my face as I realized my fingertips weren't anywhere near touching each other. Yeah, he was pretty huge.

I bit my lip when, after a slight pause, Cassian wrapped his arms around me, completely enveloping me in his arms. He smelled of wood smoke, reminding me of fireplaces and bonfires. So the scent *did* relate to their magic after all.

I pulled away after a few moments and stepped aside to let him in. He looked around the place as he walked in. "Let me guess. This is your semnyar's place."

"What gave it away? The plants or the plants?" I joked and Cassian chuckled, a deep rumbly sound that made me grin.

"Why did I always imagine you as a nerdy, video-gamer and why do you look like a jacked-up body builder?"

"Why did I always imagine you as a suave, hippie guy and why do *you* look like a nerdy video gamer?" Cassian shot back instantly and I grinned, feeling calmer than I'd felt since Rebba's call. Our friendship was pretty crazy and despite the fact that we hadn't said one thing of importance to each other yet, it was clear the discomfort we'd expected to feel on meeting face-to-face wasn't there.

"Oh, hey bud. It's nice to finally meet you." Cassian ruffled Padfoot's hair before settling down on the couch beside him, looking completely at home among the green pillows and the colorful blanket I'd been using.

Neya clambered up the plant beside the door before leaping onto my shoulder and turning her beady eyes to examine Cassian.

"Oh, hey. You're Neya, right? Please tell Raphael that Jai is worried about him but that I'm here to keep him safe and to help him with anything he needs. My name's Cassian but I think he already knows that," Cassian said the last part with a wry smirk and I wondered what that meant.

"I thought you were going to help me look for Raph?"

"I will, but he also needs to know that you're safe so he only has to worry about himself. Know what I mean?"

I nodded, feeling the exhaustion I'd been pushing away now that I had someone to lean on. I trudged over to the couch and squeezed myself into the space between my two best friends. Padfoot immediately turned over to snuggle his head in my lap.

"You look tired. Why don't you catch a nap and I'll send April to have a look around the city?"

I nodded, my eyes feeling heavier and heavier with every passing second.

"He'll be okay, Jai. Don't worry."

But how could I not? He was my boyfriend, my semnyar, my other half. I couldn't *not* worry. And I worried right up until the moment I fell asleep.

TWENTY-THREE

It was evening when I woke up and it took me a full minute to remember why I was alone in Raphael's bed and why I was still in the same clothes as yesterday. Before I could start panicking about Raph, the door opened and Cassian peeked in, smiling when he saw I was awake. He asked if he could come in and I nodded as Neya and Padfoot rushed past him and clambered up the bed, Padfoot showering me with kisses. It looked like he'd been stuck outside while I slept.

"You okay?"

I shrugged. How could I be okay? My boyfriend was missing and someone called to tell me not to worry. Oh shit.

"I forgot to tell you. A woman called me before you came to say Raph was 'working for them', whatever that meant and that they would return him when he was done. Do you think she was telling the truth?"

Cassian watched me for a moment, as if debating whether he should say whatever was on his mind. In the end he nodded and said, "I think she was. I talked to Neya a bit, well as much as I could. He's not in any danger and he doesn't want us to come get him."

I nodded, trying to make myself believe that Raph would be okay. That he would be back. His words from—was it just the day before yesterday?—popped into my head. He'd told me he would never leave me. And now, he was gone.

"Here, I made some tea for you," Cassian said, picking up a mug from the bedside table. Instead of handing it straight to me though, he held it for a moment and I watched as a small plume of steam rose above the tea.

"Here you go, nice and warm."

I chuckled despite everything, taking the now warm tea from him. "Did you seriously just use your magic to reheat my tea?"

Cassian shrugged and I shook my head as I took a sip. I was glad he was here. I was still crazy worried about Raphael but having my best friend here and having him constantly tell me that Raph was okay helped. After all, he knew more about this strange world I'd found myself in than I did. If he said Raph would be okay, I had to believe him, right?

The next four days passed with Cassian and me both staying at Raph's—his plants needed watering and I couldn't bring myself to go back to my place. I started feeling a bit more tired, not like I had way back in the beginning but still worse than I'd felt in months. It took some getting used to, but it wasn't anything new.

For the most part, we sat on the couch and talked. Cassian told me about his past and when I finally realized why everyone in Ravenshire knew him or of him—and why everyone was scared of him—my heart broke for my best friend. I hugged him to me and though he didn't shed tears, I could feel the slight shaking of his huge body as I held him. We were both such messes and I hoped that one day Cassian would find his other half too. Now, more than ever, I wanted Cassian to find his person, to find that happiness he so deserved, especially after everything he'd been through.

That night, I went to bed full of hope that Raph would be back soon and once he was, I was never letting him go anywhere. I would go wherever he went, even if I had to cuff him to me. I fell asleep quickly, thinking about everything I'd do once Raph was back.

I woke up sometime in the middle of the night with a blinding pain in my chest and I only had enough time to call out for help before the pain became too much for me and a different kind of darkness consumed me.

Raphael

"Will I really be able to play tennis again, Mister Magician?" Cam asked me, just like she had everyday since I'd first met her.

Just like every other time, I smiled at her and squeezed her hand. She already looked so much better than she had four days ago. There was color in her cheeks, she was breathing on her own and keeping down almost everything she ate. I'd probably need to work on her for another few weeks, but I was hoping that once she was mobile, I could convince William to let me go with a promise that I would visit everyday. I just hoped he'd agree because I was going crazy not getting to see my semnyar. Semnyars weren't supposed to stay away from each other for so long.

I yawned as I squeezed her hand. My sleep schedule was all screwed up since I'd started staying up with Cam so she wouldn't suffer while she was awake. It was two in the morning and she looked nowhere near ready for bed.

"Yes, sweet Cam. You'll get to—"

My words cut off as a sharp pain lanced through my chest, making me gasp as my vision wavered. What the fuck?

I didn't even realize I'd fallen off my chair until someone heaved me up, but I still couldn't find my footing, the pain in my chest taking up all my attention. The thing was, it wasn't my pain. Which meant...

A picture from Neya popped into my head and I gasped. Jai was in an ambulance, hooked up to machines. Shit. Shit. Shit.

I straightened up and stumbled when I tried to take a step, but then someone was stopping me. I needed to go. My semnyar was in pain and I had to go to him. I struggled against the arms holding me, but they were firm and unyielding.

"Let me go!" I begged, needing to get out of here. Nothing mattered except making sure my semnyar was okay.

"Daddy! Stop it!" A sweet voice called from behind me and the arms around me disappeared. I stumbled again as I tried to catch my footing and turned around to face William.

"My semnyar is in the hospital. I need to go. My powers won't work if anything happened to him, so it's in your best interest if you let me go." I said the words as calmly as I could, but inside I was screaming at him to get out of the way. Even if he said no, I'd find a way. Because Jai was more important than anything else in my life.

When William didn't say anything, I continued, "Cam will be okay for at least a month, if more. I promise to return as soon as my Jai is okay. And anyway, you know where I live, you can just pick me up again if you think I'm not coming back."

"Daddy..." Cam called from behind William and he walked over to her, caressing her cheek and completely ignoring me. Maybe I should just make a run for it. "Yes, sweetie?"

"Please let Mr. Magician go. Mr. Jai is sick like me too. He needs to help him. I want to meet Mr. Jai when I'm better and his dog, Padfoot too. I know Mr. Magician will come back. He likes hanging out with me. Right, Mr. Magician?"

I nodded as my eyes teared up, both for this sweet, selfless girl and my semnyar, who was in so much pain. "I love hanging out with you, Cam. I promise I'll come back soon."

William watched us for a moment before silently walking out of the room. An agonizingly long minute later, he was back with another man. He nodded at me. "Carter will take you to the hospital. Please don't break your promise. I'm trusting you." The way he said the words told me what he wasn't saying. He didn't trust people easily, especially when it came to his daughter, but he was willing to trust me.

I nodded and followed Carter out, wishing he'd walk faster as I followed him out of the house and to a black Audi parked in the driveway. I got in and closed my eyes, focusing on my bond with Neya as Carter started driving.

Neya sent me some soothing vibes, as if that would help me, while I watched what was happening through her eyes. They were in a room, a private room maybe? Jai was in bed, asleep or unconscious, hooked up to a million machines.

There was no one in his room, which made me frown. Had his parents not been notified? Had he been alone at our place all this time?

But then I remembered what Neya had shown me that first day. A huge man with red hair, beard and fiery orange-yellow eyes. Cassian. He was there. Jai's best friend. Thank fuck my semnyar wasn't alone. And though Cassian Romanov had a reputation in Ravenshire, and though I'd been wary of the fact that he was Jai's best friend, everything Jai had told me about him had made me realize that just like me, he was another victim of the exclusive and arrogant nature of most people in Ravenshire. I knew the man cared for my semnyar. I knew he'd keep him safe. But only I could bring him back to health and I needed to get to him.

TWENTY-FOUR

Raphael

I ran down the hallway towards Jai's room, thankful for my last name for the first time in my life. I'd told Carter to wait in the driveway for a squirrel and he'd looked acceptably confused, but I'd just told Neya through our link to get there. She would watch over Cam while I took care of Jai and let me know if anything happened. With that taken care of, I focused on getting to Jai's room.

As soon as I stepped into the hospital room, my eyes fell on my semnyar. He was surrounded by machines and tubes and it took all my control to keep the tears at bay. Shit. Jai was here because of me. I was his semnyar. I should've been there for him, should've kept him safe and healthy like I was supposed to. I shouldn't have let William convince me to stay. I'd always been unable to fight for myself. It was why I'd let my parents treat me the way they had for so long. I should've fought William because my semnyar was the most important thing in my life and I'd put everything at a risk because I was a coward.

I'd taken all of two steps towards Jai when someone grabbed me, their hand wrapping around my neck as they dragged me backward. I couldn't see them, but I could sense they were a mage. A man, judging by the strong grip on my neck. Cassian?

I found myself slammed against the wall, with a man towering over me. He had red hair and beard, and blazing orange-yellow eyes and my own widened as I realized I was right. Fuck. I should've realized he would be angry at me. And everyone from Ravenshire knew what happened when Cassian Romanov got angry.

"M-Mister Romanov?" I asked hesitantly. I knew he wouldn't hurt me—he cared for Jai and he'd never hurt him like that—but I still couldn't stop myself from shuddering in fear as I saw the fire blazing in his eyes.

It seemed like he realized what he was doing because he pulled back suddenly, making me gasp in a huge breath as he shook his head before crossing his arms over his chest and standing between me and my semnyar, looking for all the world like a hired muscle intent on keeping Jai safe. If it was anyone else, I would have been furious, but I knew Cassian only meant to protect my semnyar and for that I was grateful to him. And yes, I was a little bit scared of him too.

"What the fuck kind of man leaves their semnyar without a word, especially when you knew how much he needed you?"

I rubbed my palm over my face, my whole body yearning to be close to Jai, to give him all of my magic just so he'd wake up but I knew I needed to tell Cassian something before he let me.

"I was uh-kidnapped. Someone at the hospital told someone about my powers and he wanted me to heal his daughter. I couldn't say no because she was just a kid and dying. I had to help. He wouldn't let me contact anyone, so I couldn't talk to Jai. Neya stayed with him for my peace of mind, so when

I realized what had happened, I told the father I could either leave and return or I wouldn't be able to heal his daughter. Camille convinced him to let me go, so here I am."

Cassian watched me for a moment before nodding stiffly and stepping back. I hurried to Jai's side, taking the hard plastic chair and grabbing his hand as soon as I was seated.

"I'm so sorry, baby. I'm so sorry," I mumbled as I let my magic flow. His heart seemed like it was forcing every beat and I focused my magic on it, letting it slowly ease the way.

I didn't know how long I pushed my magic into him, but I didn't stop even when I felt my well depleting. I'd never felt that before and any other time, I would've stopped to give myself time to refill, but not right now. My semnyar needed me and I would give him the last drop of my magic if that's what I needed to do.

Maybe I did just that, or maybe the strain got to be too much for me, because after a few moments I found myself slowly sinking into darkness. I didn't mind. As long as Jai was okay, I didn't mind at all.

Jai

My eyes fluttered open and as the beeping sound registered in my mind, I realized I'd woken up in a hospital. That wasn't surprising in itself. I'd woken up in a hospital many times. What was surprising was how good I felt. Nothing felt wrong, so why was I here?

My head snapped to the side as I realized why I must be feeling so well and sure enough, a familiar blond head rested on my hand, face down with his hair splayed all over the place. I smiled despite the million questions running around my head. My semnyar was here. Everything would be okay now.

I pulled my hand away to run my fingers through his hair, expecting him to wake up. When he didn't, I shook his shoulder gently. "Raph? Angel?"

When he still didn't wake up, I started panicking. What was wrong? Why wouldn't he wake up?

"Hey, J. He's okay," A familiar voice spoke up from my other side and I looked over to see Cassian standing there, dressed in the same clothes he'd been in when I'd last seen him.

"Why won't he wake up?" I gasped out, finding it harder and harder to breathe as I wondered what was wrong.

"He's okay. He just overexerted himself while trying to heal you."

"Oh. So he'll be okay?" I asked, turning back to look at my angel.

"Yeah, he'll be fine. Don't worry."

I nodded, running my fingers through Raph's hair as I thought about what I wanted to ask next. "Did he...did he tell you where he'd been?"

"Yeah, he said he was kidnapped by some guy who wanted him to heal his daughter. Said she was young so he couldn't just leave and decided to help her. Apparently, the man wouldn't let him contact you."

I smiled softly as I thought over what Cassian had said. Of course Raph couldn't leave. He'd been right to stay too, if his staying meant another kid was saved from a half-life like mine or death. I just wished I'd known, that I hadn't spent the last few days worrying or wondering if he'd had enough of me too.

"You're not mad at him?" Cassian asked and I looked at him to find him watching me with a puzzled look in his pretty fire eyes. Did all mages have beautiful eyes?

I shook my head as I tried to remember what he'd asked. "Oh, no. Not at all. He was saving a kid's life. How can I be mad at him for that? Though yes, I am mad at the man who took him. Why couldn't he have just asked Raph like a normal person? I know there's no way he would've said no."

"Maybe the man has trust issues. Or maybe he did think he would say no," Cass offered and I shrugged. It didn't matter now. Raph was here and if he needed to go back to help the girl, I would go with him. There was no way I was letting him leave my side for even a minute now.

"Where're my parents?"

"It's the middle of the night, so I didn't want to bother them. I left them a text instead. They should be here once they wake up, I think."

"You didn't have to do that," I said, looking up at him. He'd really come through for me. Despite his wish to never meet face to face—though I guessed that had mostly been because of the mage thing—the moment I'd needed him, he'd shown up, no complaints. From what Raph had said, he was an extremely private person and hadn't left the island in decades. Yet, he'd made the trip for me. That in itself was more than I'd ever expected from him.

Cassian smiled softly at me, his eyes reminding me of a comfy fireplace and said, "I know that, but I wanted to. You're a great friend, Jai. And I'm glad this idiot is your semnyar because I'd been dreading the day I might lose you. Now you'll live as long as us, so I don't have to worry about it."

I grinned at him, shaking my head. I believed him though, mostly because I couldn't imagine losing him as a friend either. Knowing what I knew of his life, I knew he'd been just as lonely as me. Now that he was here, I was determined to make sure he returned and kept visiting. He didn't have to live the hermit life anymore.

"Where's April?" I asked when I remembered his trusty owl familiar.

"Back at your place with Padfoot and your brother. I texted him separately and apparently, he was awake. So he offered to pet sit while I brought you here."

"And Neya?"

Cassian's brows furrowed as he thought about it before shaking his head, "No clue. She was here until a few minutes ago."

"She's with Cam," Raph said and I almost got whiplash with how quickly I turned to face him. He was rubbing his eyes like a sleepy kid and I smiled at his adorableness.

"Cam?" Cassian asked from behind me.

"The girl I was healing," Raph said as his eyes finally met mine, relief, love and...fear shining through them. What was he scared of?

I opened my arms slightly, careful of the IV and he made a choking sound before scrambling into my arms without putting his weight on me. "Oh mother, Jai. I'm so sorry. I'm sorry."

"Shh..." I murmured soothingly when I realized he was shaking. I rubbed his back as he buried his face in my neck. I could feel his tears and I had to hold back my own because he needed to see that I was okay.

"Hey, I'm okay. Don't worry. And honestly, if you'd left that little girl without healing her, I would've been very angry. You did the right thing, Angel."

"But you got sick because of me."

"No, sweetie. I'm getting better because of you. If this had happened before I met you, I'd probably be dead right now."

Raph's whole body jerked in my arms as he gasped. "Don't say that."

"It's the truth, Angel. I'm alive because of you, okay?"

He pulled back to stare into my eyes for a moment and I brought my hand up to wipe away his tears as he nodded.

Leaning forward, I pressed a kiss to the tip of his nose, making him smile.

"Alright, quit the lovefest. Now, Raphael, do I need to go threaten this man so he doesn't take you again or are you done with him?"

Raph tilted his head thoughtfully as he met my eyes. "I do need to go back, but I told him I'll come back on my own once I was sure Jai was okay."

Cassian was watching me, waiting for my reaction. Though Cassian had never been anything but sweet with me, he had a rugged sort of appearance that paired with his fire magic definitely made him look threatening. I was also angry at this man for kidnapping my semnyar, so I grinned at Cass as I spoke, "How about you maybe pay him a visit to make sure he knows he can't keep my semnyar away from me again?"

Cassian grinned, obviously happy with my decision while Raph chuckled on my other side. "Give me the address, *Angel* and I'll see to it that he knows the score."

I bristled at Cassian's use of my nickname for Raph but he just winked at me which made Raph grumble. Shaking my head, I lay back on the bed, feeling content now that my other half was right where he should be. With me.

A few hours later, my parents showed up with hot tea and breakfast and Raph looked adorably shocked when Ma hugged him and I just winked at him. I hadn't told my parents about his disappearance because I hadn't wanted to worry them and I was glad I hadn't.

Raph fed me breakfast even though I was completely capable of eating on my own. Actually, once I had a chance to really look him over, I realized he looked even more exhausted than I did. And had he lost weight? Was that even possible in the short time he'd been away from me?

"Why do you look so exhausted?" I asked once we'd finished eating. Cassian had left to visit a certain William Hawthorne, while my parents had gone to talk to Dr.Merryweather, so we were alone for the moment.

Raph shrugged but when I just kept staring at him, he sighed. "I spent a lot of time healing Cam so I could get back quicker. I guess it took a toll on me."

I frowned as I brought his hand up to kiss the back of it. There was no way I was letting him go back there alone. No way at all. "I'm coming with you when you go there."

"But—"

"No," I cut him off as I tucked his unruly hair behind his ear, "I can't stay away from you like this again, Angel. I can't take it."

Raph watched me for a moment before nodding. "Alright, but only once you're feeling better."

"Right back at you. You need a break too."

"Deal."

TWENTY-FIVE

Jai

"Stop fussing, Raph," I said as I watched Raphael flutter around the room with no goal in mind. He grabbed a corner of the blanket he'd covered me with and untucked it before tucking it back in. Ugh, he was driving me crazy.

"Raph! Come here," I ordered, my voice firm. His eyes widened before he walked closer to the bed. I lifted the covers and jerked my head towards the space beside me. He opened his mouth to protest and I narrowed my eyes. With a huff, he climbed in, snuggling closer to me as soon as he was under the covers.

After we got back from the hospital, Cass and Joy had taken Padfoot and the other fur babies out for a stroll—and in case of April, a flight—leaving the two of us alone at Raph's place. Without wasting a minute, Raph had almost carried me into the bedroom and bundled me up in blankets. He'd been fussing ever since, vibrating with an unending energy for the last twenty minutes or so.

"Calm down, Angel. I'm fine, okay? I woke up feeling better than I have in the past few days. Whatever was wrong with me, you worked your magic on it."

"Whatever was wrong? Didn't the doctor tell you?" Raph demanded and he would've sat up if I hadn't managed to wrap my arms and legs around him.

"Uh, we kinda came home before he got there? I'm pretty sure it was just stress though. I'm fine, Raph. You can see it for yourself if you want."

Raph watched me for a moment before nodding. "You'll tell me if you start feeling off?"

I nodded, happy that he was willing to believe me.

"Now, you need some sleep because honestly, you look worse than me. I'll be right here, wrapped around you, but I want you to get some sleep, okay? You wouldn't be able to help the little girl if you aren't at your best. I don't want you killing yourself over this."

Raphael opened his mouth again and I pressed my mouth to his to keep him quiet. I kissed him sweetly, softly because even as a part of me yearned to get rid of all the clothes and claim him after being away from each other for what felt like years, a bigger part of me wanted to take care of my semnyar like he always took care of me.

I pulled back, giving his lips another peck before pulling him closer. I ran my fingers through his hair as he snuggled against my chest and within minutes, his breathing calmed and I could hear his soft snores muffled against my chest.

A few minutes later, my bedroom door opened and Cassian peeked in. He opened his mouth and I pressed my own finger to my lips to shush him, pointing at the lump under the blankets beside me.

Cass grinned, nodding and I followed his eyes as he looked down at Padfoot who was trying to nose his way into the room. I bit back a chuckle and gave him a short nod and he opened the door further.

Padfoot wasted no time hopping up on the bed and showering me with love, trying his best to lick my face as he tried to show me how much he'd missed me. "I missed you too, my big bad husky. But we gotta be quiet, yeah? Daddy Raph is sleeping."

Padfoot watched me with his pretty blue eyes before walking over to the free space on the other side of Raph and laying down, his body pressed against Raph's. I smiled at him, leaning over to ruffle his fur and he snuffled before sinking down on the bed and closing his eyes.

I looked back to see Cass still standing in the doorway and he smiled at me when he met my eyes. He made a motion with his hand that seemed an awful lot like *I'm gonna head out*. My eyes widened and I shook my head. No way was he leaving so soon.

I grabbed my phone and first texted Joy his new mission: Don't let Cass leave.

Then I texted Cass, even though he was standing right there.

Me: Don't you dare leave just yet.

Cass: I did what I came to. Do you need help with something else?

Me: NO! I just want to hang out with my best friend without the threat over my semnyar hanging over my head. One more day, please?

Cass huffed and I looked up at him just in time to catch his nod. I smiled at him and blew him a kiss, which made him roll his eyes. He hooked his thumb behind him towards the direction of the living room and I nodded.

Cassian closed the door behind him and I went back to watching Raph as he slept beside me, thanking all the gods my Ma prayed to that he was okay.

Raphael

I watched Jai while he ate and I knew I was annoying him, but I'd missed my semnyar and I'd thought he was going to die because of me. I deserved to gawk at him. Plus, it wasn't like he could keep his eyes away from me anyway. Even as he chatted with Cassian—who was heading back to Ravenshire tomorrow with the promise of visiting often—his eyes kept trailing back to me and I wasn't even trying to hide the fact that I was watching him as we ate dinner.

Joy had left earlier since he had school tomorrow and I was glad he wasn't too shaken up about everything. Apparently, this hadn't been the first time Jai had to be hospitalized in the middle of the night. I was hoping it would be the last though, because I had zero plans of ever letting him out of my sight again. Which meant I needed to talk to Jai about moving in soon.

Once dinner was done, Cassian insisted on cleaning up despite our protests so I dried while he washed and soon enough, it was time for bed. Cassian and his semlee, April retreated to the guest bedroom he'd been occupying for the past few days and I took Jai's hand as we walked to—hopefully—*our* room.

We brushed our teeth together and once we were back in bed, I wrapped myself around my semnyar, wishing I could stay like that all the time.

"You know," I started to speak, my fingers tracing the skin just over the edge of his collar. "The day they took me...I had a whole plan."

"A plan?" Jai asked as his fingers sank into my hair and started massaging slowly. I blinked back the tears in my eyes as I savored the touch. I'd missed that so much the past few days. I didn't regret helping Cam but I'd hated the fact that I had to stay away from my semnyar to do that.

"Mmm hmm." I cleared my throat as I looked up at him to find his gorgeous brown eyes already on me. "I was going to adopt Coop and gift him to you. I know you've wanted to adopt him for a while and I was going to get him and then ask you..." I swallowed, my voice drifting off. Jai nodded at me, urging me to go on and I took a deep breath. "I was going to ask you if you wanted to raise him together."

I bit my lip as his brows furrowed before his eyes widened in realization. I held my breath as a slow smile spread across his face and his arms tightened around my waist. "Were you going to ask me to move in with you?"

I nodded and after taking another deep breath, I popped the question. "Will you move in with me, Jai?"

Still smiling, he shook his head. "Nope."

My heart fell and the lump in my throat had me swallowing repeatedly and futilely. No? Maybe it was too soon. That had to be it, right? Humans had all these weird notions about right times and too soon and whatnot.

"You're so cute," Jai murmured and I looked up at him to find him grinning widely at me. "I can't move in with you, my sweet sweet angel, because I've already moved in with you. Do you remember the last time I stayed the night at mine while you were here?"

I thought about it and shook my head when I couldn't remember it. And then everything he'd said trickled into my slow moving brain and my eyes widened. "We're living together?"

Jai nodded and I barely stopped myself from squealing as I launched myself at him, kissing any and every part of his skin that I could get my lips on. I was going to live forever with my semnyar by my side. What more could I ask for?

"Do you want to get a bigger house?" I loved this place, but if Jai wanted a bigger place, he would get one.

"No! I love this place and I want to make a lot more memories in yo-our backyard."

I couldn't stop the tears this time but Jai didn't make me feel like I was weak or stupid for crying. Instead, he joined in and we spent a few minutes just wiping each other's happy tears.

Once I had no more tears left, I closed my eyes and snuggled deeper into Jai's chest. Wrapping my arms tightly around him, I breathed in his chocolate scent. I was home.

***

I woke up the next morning to find Jai watching me, a soft smile on his face. I shifted upwards so we were eye to eye, moaning when his morning wood rubbed against my thigh.

I blamed my sleepiness for the question that popped out of my mouth next because that could be the only reason for such stupidity. "Why are you always so quiet when we're making love?"

I knew some people were naturally quiet, but I'd seen Jai bite off or swallow his moans way too many times to believe that was the case. I didn't know why the question decided to pop out *now*, but I figured I'd roll with it now that it was out there.

His eyes widened and then he chuckled, shaking his head. "Where did *that* come from?"

I shrugged, wondering if that was all I'd get but then he rolled his eyes and spoke, "Well, it's a habit I haven't managed to let go of, I guess."

"A habit?"

"Well, until last year I lived with my parents. Their house has pretty thin walls so…"

"Oh…Ooooh…" I chuckled as I realized what he was getting at. I hadn't had the same problem because my parents were never home and even if they were, our house was huge and our rooms on opposite ends. The thought of my semnyar forcing himself to stay quiet while he pleasured himself…it was equal parts amusing and arousing.

Jai looked way too flustered though, so I leaned up on my elbow to peck his lips. I didn't intend to do more—because morning breath, duh—but Jai pulled me closer, his lips claiming mine in an intense, breathtaking kiss that had me trying to hump the air within seconds. Jai pulled up to look at me before he kicked off the blankets and straddled me. My eyes shot to the door because I knew we weren't alone, but Jai gripped my chin and tilted my head so he could kiss me again. "Cassian's out on a walk with Pads." He murmured against my lips before kissing me again.

I nodded and gasped as Jai's hand plunged into my sleep pants. I groaned when his palm wrapped around my dick pumping it once, twice, before he pulled it out of my pants. I didn't see when he got his own dick out but suddenly his palms were wrapped around the both of us and I gripped his hip as he pumped us, a steady pace that had me pushing up in an attempt to go faster.

I grabbed the back of Jai's neck and pulled him down, using my other hand to steady him as he kept pumping us. I kissed him for all I was worth and he gave back as good as he got. I loved this man more than anyone or anything else, and I wanted him to know that.

I could feel my orgasm racing in and I pulled back to look into my semnyar's eyes as I fell off the edge, my back arching upwards as I shot streams of cum up mine and Jai's body. He groaned over me, a sweet filthy sound as he emptied all over me before slumping down, both of us too tired to hold him up.

We lay there, stuck together and it took us a long few minutes to come back to the planet earth. After a few minutes, Jai looked up, resting his chin on my sternum as he gave me a soft, sated smile. "I still want Coop."

I laughed as I wrapped my arms around him and squeezed as tightly as I could without hurting him. My mate would get everything he wanted, including enough animals to turn this house into a zoo if he so wished.

"Then you'll get him. Now, let's go shower. Are you feeling well enough to visit Cam? I won't heal her much, I promise, but she's a cutie and she was worried about you. Plus, she wants to meet Pads."

Jai smiled, tucking my hair behind my ear. "I'll go anywhere as long as it's with you. Now let's get into the shower before Cass gets back. We're close but not enough that I'd want him to get a peek at my ass."

I growled as I sat up, Jai still in my arms and he giggled—I repeat, *giggled*—as I carried him into the bathroom. It was the most beautiful sound I'd ever heard.

TWENTY-SIX

Raphael

The drive to William's mansion on the other end of the city took nearly forty minutes. Jai had insisted Cassian stay at least till this evening, so Cassian had in turn insisted on coming with us. So now, the big redhead was stuffed into the backseat with Padfoot, April and Neya. For some reason, my semlee wanted to hang around his neck. I swear I saw her nibbling at his beard a minute ago.

Jai was driving so I had all the time I needed to tease Cassian about this sudden interest all the animals had in him. I adored Cassian, for what he'd done for my semnyar and for everything he'd been through. Of course, I wouldn't tell him that, but he was pretty damn cute under all that exterior. I could bet that he would act like an overprotective papa bear the moment he found his semnyar. I hoped he'd find his other half soon, he'd been alone long enough. He'd suffered enough.

"Okay, we're here!" Jai declared just as the GPS lady repeated his sentiment in her own words.

Jai was out of the door before I could tell him to wait for me and I shook my head as I got out. He was opening the back door and clipping on Padfoot's leash as I walked over. Once he was done, I took his hand in mine, giving it a squeeze. He looked up at me with a smile, his other hand wrapped around Padfoot's leash and we walked towards the front door. I could feel Cassian standing just behind us, and I knew without looking that he had a scowl on his face as he looked around, intimidating anyone who dared look at us. See, Papa Bear right there.

The door was opened by Miss Avery, William's PA. William had moved his work to his home so he could be there for his daughter and his PA had more or less taken over the household. I sensed a low-key romance brewing, to be honest.

"Mr. Woodward," She greeted before her eyes fell on Cassian and narrowed slightly.

"Hey Avery, this is my boyfriend, Jai Presley. And our friend, Cassian Romanov. Is Cam up?"

Avery nodded a hello to Jai before turning to me. "Oh yes, she's been worried about you and Mr. Presley. Come on in. I'll let William know you're here."

We followed her into the living room and while she disappeared around the right hallway, I led Jai down the left, eager to see Cam and hopeful that my absence hadn't pushed her progress back.

"Here's her room. You ready?" I asked Jai and he nodded. I turned to Cassian, who still looked like a grumbly bear and tsked. "Change your face and try not to scare her."

Cassian gave me a wide-eyed look that almost looked comical. "What?"

I waved my hand towards his face, shaking my head in emphasis. "That. Stop doing that to your face. Be smiley. We're meeting an eight year old girl, not the Inquisition."

Jai giggled and I grinned at him before knocking on the door and peeking inside. Cam was sitting up in her bed, a book in her tiny hands but she looked up the moment I peeked in, a bright smile lighting up her face. "Mr. Magician!"

I opened the door and ushered everyone in, leaving it open behind us as I walked towards the bed and gave Cam a gentle hug. "Hey, Cam! How are you?"

Camille completely ignored my question as her eyes fell on Padfoot and she gave the husky a wave, giggling when the dog tried to hop up on the bed to greet her. I grabbed his leash from Jai so he wouldn't topple over and chided Pads gently, "Calm down, Padfoot."

"His name is Padfoot? Like from the Harry Potter movies?" Cam asked and Jai grinned, nodding his head as he walked closer to the little girl and extended his hand.

"Yep, you guessed it right. Hey Cam, my name's Jai and it's very nice to meet you."

"You're Mr. Magician's boyfriend, right? Are you okay now? He said you were sick."

"I'm alright now, sweetie. Mr. Magician worked his magic on me."

"Good," Cam declared. She looked around and her eyes fell on Cassian who looked like he was trying to become one with the wall.

"Wow. Your eyes are so pretty. Can I see them up close?" Cam asked and I bit back a chuckle at the wide-eyes, almost scared look on Cassian's face. Seems like I'd found the one thing that could scare him.

"Yes, Cassian show her your pretty eyes," I said, nudging him with my elbow and sliding away before he could reciprocate.

Cassian glared at me before turning to Cam with a small smile. He walked closer to Cam, April on his shoulder and gave her an awkward wave. "Hey, my name's Cassian."

"Are you magic too? Mr. Magician has pretty eyes and he can do magic," Cam informed him and he nodded as if it was news to him. He looked back at me with pleading eyes and I shrugged, enjoying watching him squirm way too much.

He turned back to Cam and extended his index finger, palm up and after a beat, a tiny flame hovered over his finger, orange-yellow like his eyes. Cam's eyes widened and she clapped her hands as she stared at the flame. "Can I touch it?"

Cassian shook his head, extinguishing the flame quickly before giving her a strained smile. "You'll get burnt, little girl."

Cam nodded, taking him at his word. She looked up at him and her eyes fell on the eagle-owl on his shoulder. I'd honestly expected her to spot April first, but she'd been distracted by the pretty eyes, apparently.

"Wow. That's a big bird. Is it yours?"

Cassian nodded, smiling sweetly as he extended his arm and April hopped over to the leather brace on his forearm. "Her name is April."

Cam extended a hand hesitantly and petted April, who puffed up in pleasure, chirping softly.

"Alrighty, let's get to work so you can be all better soon, okay Cam?" I asked, dragging my chair from the corner of the room to her bedside. She looked at me with wide eyes, biting her lip.

"Will you visit me after I'm healthy again, Mr. Magician?"

"Of course, sweetie. I'll be there at all of your tennis matches. You can come to our house too. We have a huge tree in our backyard that you can climb." Cam grinned at my reply, extending her hand.

Cassian moved away from the bed to give me space and I took Cam's hand in mine, closing my eyes as I let my magic scan her. Her lungs were doing well, no more unwanted fluids there. A few more sessions and she'd be completely healthy.

I focused my magic on the pains and aches first, before pushing deeper to the tumors and dead cells, breaking them and burning them off with my magic. I still wasn't a hundred percent sure how my magic worked. We usually didn't have spells. All we needed to do was make our intentions clear and bam. According to my mother, we needed to make our intentions clearer than *I want to heal her* to make them work. But for some reason, my magic was instinctual.

William arrived just as I was finishing up and his eyes narrowed at the crowd, especially once he spotted Cassian. The wariness in his eyes told me Cassian had kept his promise to Jai.

William turned to me with a raised brow. "Was it really necessary to bring your bodyguard here?"

"Oh daddy, don't be crazy. He's Mr. Magician's friend. He can do magic too."

"And as for being Raph's bodyguard," Jai said, narrowing his eyes and stalking towards William with a determined look in his eyes, "you're lucky you have a sweet daughter who needs you and my boyfriend, or you'd have some serious issues. How dare you just pick him up off the street like that? Do you have any clue how worried we were? Would it really have been so much trouble to ask him for help? Or was that too much for your ego?"

William stared back at Jai and I was out of my seat before he finished speaking, sliding up beside Jai and wrapping my arm around his waist. My semnyar was small, but he looked like he could do some serious damage right now. I'd never seen him so angry before.

William watched Jai for a minute before his shoulders slumped and he backed away. "You're right, I'm sorry. I know I should've gone differently about this but..." he stopped speaking to glance up at Cam who was watching everything with a troubled look on her face. He walked over to her, kissing her cheek. "We'll be in the living room, 'kay Cammy?"

She looked at me, her lower lip pushing out in a pout. "You'll be back, right?"

"Of course, Cam," I promised her and she looked up at her dad with a smile and nodded.

Maneuvering slowly, we all made our way to the living room. I hadn't been in this room much while I was here, just my room, Cam's and the kitchen. The room was huge, with a high ceiling, large windows that looked out over the property and leather couches laid around a dark wooden coffee table. A large flat-screen covered one wall and a tall bookshelf sat beside an electric fireplace. One look at Jai and I grinned as I found him doing exactly what I'd expected: looking over the titles of the book. According to Jai, you could tell a lot about people from the books they read.

Jai looked up at William as he sat down across from us, Cassian preferring to stand with his hip leaning against the couch. No wonder he looked like a bodyguard.

"You were saying?" Jai prompted and William gave him a sheepish smile, running his fingers through his hair.

"The day I had Raphael...picked up, Cam's doctor told me that she only had a week or two at the most. I lost her mother when she was just a baby, but Veronica made me promise to keep our daughter safe and I'd promised her I would. I loved Veronica and I love Cam. I can't imagine my life without

Cam. She is the only reason I'm still here. So I may have gone a bit...crazy when I got the news. Now that she is better, I can see how irrational I'd been and I'm really sorry for the inconvenience. I'll pay you double what I intended. I know it's not the same thing. I can't take away the pain I caused you, but I hope you'll accept it."

I opened my mouth to tell him that I didn't need the extra money, he'd already been paying me well-enough, but Jai squeezed my hand and nodded. "I can understand what you went through. Not exactly how it was for you, but I've watched my parents make enough bad decisions over my health to know how you must've felt. We'll be back for the next session tomorrow."

William nodded and I got up as Jai did, tugging Pads with me as we headed outside. I smiled at William over my shoulder. "Don't worry, she'll be perfectly healthy in a few weeks or so."

His eyes glittered as he nodded at me, mouthing the words thank you. I gave him another smile as I shrugged my shoulders before turning around and following my semnyar down the front steps.

Once back in the car, I turned to Jai and asked the question bubbling in my mind. "Why didn't you want me to decline the money?"

Jai grinned as he started the car and drove around the circular driveway. "Well, we're going to live forever, right? I don't know about you, but I'd like to have some extra pocket money to spend. Maybe get a few more animals or start a charity or go on a trip. But more than that...I wanted to pay my parents back. I know it's technically your money, but if you don't mind, I'd like to give some of it to my parents. They've spent a lot over the years to keep me alive and I want them to have a bit more security for when they're older."

"Jai, what's mine is yours, okay? And I agree. Your parents are awesome and they deserve to live in luxury."

"Thanks, Raph. I love you."

"I love you, too, baby."

"Ugh, cut the sappy shit out, you two," Cassian grumbled from the back seat and we burst out laughing. Damn, life was good, wasn't it?

Jai

"Come on, baby boy. Your dinner's served," I called out and Padfoot came racing off the couch where he'd been dozing on and off since we got home and being the lazy brat he was. He woofed at me and I ruffled his fur and pointed at his bowl in a *have at it* motion. Wagging his tail, Pads headed over to his dinner and I turned towards the counter to figure out what we were having for dinner now that His Highness had been served.

Warm arms wrapped around me and Raph rested his chin on top of my head. "Let's order in tonight. I wanna cuddle and watch a movie. What do you say?"

I hummed as I leaned back into him, closing my eyes as the familiar scent of honey and grass enveloped my senses. "Sounds good. What movie do you wanna watch?"

"How about...*Deadpool 2*?"

"Again?"

Raph shrugged against me and I rolled my eyes as I turned around in his arms and met his green-brown eyes. "Why don't you just admit you have a huge crush on Ryan Reynolds?"

"I have eyes only for you, my dearest," Raph proclaimed, deepening his voice and puffing out his chest. I couldn't help laughing at his antics. He was way too adorable.

"Yeah, yeah. I'm already yours. No need to butter me up."

He gasped, placing a palm against his chest and looking oh-so-wounded. "Why, I'd never!"

I chuckled, which turned into a laugh and soon we were both laughing like crazy while Padfoot danced around our feet, wanting to join in on the fun, his food already gone. Cassian had left just a few minutes ago with a promise to visit soon and I knew he'd be back. I was looking forward to having more of him in my life. Plus, he really needed to get out more. If anything good had come out of this whole debacle, it had been the fact that I got to meet my best friend in person.

I wiped the tears of mirth from my eyes and straightened up from where I'd ended up leaning against the counter for support. It still surprised me how *not* out of breath I was after a huge round of laughter like that. Before, it'd have left me with burning lungs and tears of pain in my eyes, but now I felt the barest of twinges in my chest and nothing else.

"Alright. You order the food, I'll put on the movie," I said once I was sure we were all laughed out. I leaned up to give Raph a peck on his lips before moving into the living area and switching on the TV.

By the time I had the movie up and ready to play, Raph was back with Neya on his shoulder. I got comfortable on the couch and curled my legs under me, grabbing the blanket Raphael had made off the back of the couch and covering us once he was seated beside me. I was looking forward to moving the rest of my stuff into this home and making it *ours*. Hopefully, we'd do it soon. I also wanted to ask Raph something else, a question that had been burning in my mind more and more recently. I wasn't sure how Raph would answer it, but I hoped it wouldn't be a no. It *couldn't* be a no, right?

We huddled closer as I hit play and though I knew one of us would have to get up when the food arrived, I wrapped myself around my mate, breathing in his scent as the opening credits started playing on the screen. I'd missed this the past few days, missed the comfort and peace I found in his arms. I was never letting him get away from me ever again.

The doorbell rang only a few minutes later, making me huff in surprise. "Woah, that was quick. Did they send leftovers or something?" I joked as I started to get out of the comfortable cocoon I'd made around us, but Raphael beat me to it.

"I'll get it, baby. Keep my space warm." Raph winked at me before walking over to the door and I hit pause as I waited for him. Gods forbid he should miss a scene with his crush being all badass.

I heard the door open and then...silence. I was just about to ask what was wrong when Raph's voice floated over to me, sounding hoarse and raw. "Mother?"

My eyes widened and I struggled to get out of the damned couch, my legs tangling up in the blanket. As soon as I'd untangled myself, I was at Raph's side, glaring at the woman who'd given birth to him.

She looked...plain. Nothing like the bright and beautiful person that was Raphael. She looked like she was in her early thirties—yeah, right—and her blond hair was tied off in a tight bun, stretching her forehead wide. Her lips were pursed into some semblance of a smile that looked more like a grimace and she wore a dark pink pant-suit. Suddenly, the image of Umbridge from *Harry Potter* popped into my head and I nodded sagely. Yep, that was the exact same bitch face.

"Raphael, son, you weren't taking my calls so I had to track you down. Now that you've finally figured out what your powers mean, don't you think you'd be better off at Ravenshire, working with us at the hospital instead of living...here?" The note of derision in her voice raised my hackles even further and my hands curled into fists at my side.

I looked up at Raph, wanting to make sure he was okay, to find his face pale and drawn. I grabbed his hand and gave it a reassuring squeeze and he met my eyes. Silently, I asked him to let me do the caring for once. To let me take care of him like he'd taken care of me from the very beginning. He nodded subtly and I smiled at him before taking a step that put me between the mother and son.

"Okay, Mrs. Woodward. Here's the thing. I want to call you a lot of names and tell you a lot of things that I probably shouldn't even think about my semnyar's mother, but you deserve it. Your son is an amazing man, and I'm not saying that because he's my semnyar. He's amazing, beautiful and so full of love, love that he gives me freely. He'd wanted to love you too, but how long can you love a person when all they do is treat your love—and you—like it's nothing? You had a hundred and fifty years to show him you loved him, but you didn't. You can't just come knocking and expect him to come back after everything you and that goddamn island full of mages put him through."

Bitch face opened her mouth to say something but I cut her off. "I'm not finished. Raphael is happy here. He has his semlee and his semnyar. He has a job he loves and a house he adores. You're nothing to him anymore and I'm warning you to never contact him again. If he wants to make amends, he will come to you. I know you might be thinking what a human like me could do if you didn't heed it and you'd be right. But the thing is, my best friend cares about me a lot. And he'd gladly help me out. I've been told he's pretty famous over in Ravenshire. Cassian Romanov?" I didn't feel the tiniest speck of remorse at throwing my best friend's name around like that. He'd shown me over the last few days that though he was completely unlike the intimidating persona he showed others, he didn't mind doing so to protect the people he cared about. And he'd pretty much told me to feel free to use his name in not so many words. I believed his words to me had been *I don't mind living up to my reputation if it is to keep the ones I care about from harm.*

Bitch face's eyes widened and I smirked, satisfied my hunch had been right. She knew exactly who Cassian was and she was afraid of him. "Exactly. So get out and never, ever come near us again. Got it?"

Bitch face huffed, shooting a glare over my shoulder before turning on her heels and making her way down the driveway. The food delivery arrived just then, so I paid for it and closed the door before turning to face Raph. He stood right where he'd been the entire time and I placed the food on the kitchen counter before walking over and pulling him into my arms.

"I didn't overdo it, did I?" I murmured, pressing a kiss against his chin.

Raph shook his head but stayed silent and I rubbed his back, hoping he'd be okay. After a few minutes of holding me, he pulled back and gave me a bright, sincere smile. "Thank you for doing that for me. I feel so much...lighter now. I didn't realize how much she was dragging me down until now. I feel...free. And safe. So, thank you."

I leaned up on my toes and pulled him into a kiss, showing him just how much I loved him. I'd do anything to keep him safe, be it standing up against an egoistic bitch or throwing my fire-mage best friend's name around to scare people. My angel always came first.

"Come on, we've got a movie to watch, remember?" I led him towards the couch, grabbing the pizza boxes from the counter on my way there. We got back under the blanket and I hit play, smiling at Raph as he grinned at whatever new antics *Deadpool* was up to. I had my semnyar with me and nothing felt better than cuddling on the couch and watching movies with him, safe in our little cocoon with forever on the horizon. I couldn't wait to spend forever with my angel.

EPILOGUE

We stayed on the couch even after the movie ended, empty pizza boxes lying on the coffee table as we lazed in each other's arms. I tilted my head up to look at Raph, tucking my chin on his chest as my arms tightened around him.

"Hey, Angel?"

"Hmm?" Raph mumbled, eyes closed as his palm stroked my back, dipping under my shirt every other time and caressing my skin and making goosebumps pop up all over.

"We're forever, right? This bond we share, it's forever, yes?"

Raph opened his eyes to smile at me, his hand coming up to rest against my cheek. "Yes, it is."

I nodded. "So, I know you probably don't need it...or maybe you won't even want to, but..." I trailed off, blowing out a heavy breath while I wondered if I was being stupid. I already had him, would it really change things so much? Was it even necessary?

"But what?"

I'd closed my eyes but then snapped them open again so I would know he wasn't just saying yes to make me happy. "I know I'm already your semnyar and you're mine, but...would you like to be my husband?"

Raph's eyes widened and he sat up, pulling me closer before I could fall. He gripped my face between his palms and looked into my eyes. "Are you asking me to marry you, Jai?"

I nodded, swallowing hard before asking him as steadily as I could, my heart beating wildly against my rib cage. At that moment, I knew even Raph's magic wouldn't be able to calm it down. "Will you marry me, Angel? You're my semnyar, my soulmate and my other half. Will you be my husband too?"

Tears glittered in his eyes as he pulled me closer and slammed his lips against mine, kissing me with so much love and adoration that it left me breathless as I scrambled around and straddled him, my fingers sinking into his hair and holding on as he explored every inch of my mouth as if he was kissing me for the first time.

When we were both breathless, he pulled away, resting his forehead against mine as we tried to suck in enough oxygen to appease our lungs. "Was that a yes?" I gasped out as soon as I could and Raph chuckled.

"Of course it was a yes. But I have one condition."

"Anything."

Raph smiled at me, kissing my lips softly and speaking against them. "I love your family and I want to be a part of them. I want to be Raphael Presley."

I smiled at him, tucking his unruly hair behind his ear as I took in this man who'd breezed into my life just a few short months ago and changed it so completely. With a single touch of magic, he'd shown me the world. And now he was all mine, my mate and soon my husband.

"Raphael Presley. Sounds perfect," I murmured and he kissed me again, softer this time. His arms wrapped around me and he stood up, somehow untangling himself from the blankets without letting me go.

We kissed like we had all the time in the world and wasn't that the truth?

I was just about to ask him to set me down so we could clean up quickly and move this into the bedroom when there was a knock at the door. I pulled back with a frown, wondering if Mrs. Bitch Face was back. I swore I'd end up seriously hurting her if she didn't leave my boyfr-no, my fiancé alone.

"Let me," I said and Raph did, letting me slide down his body so I knew exactly what he had in mind for later and exactly how much he was looking forward to it.

I shot him a mock glare as I adjusted my own visible hardness so it wasn't quite as noticeable before heading over to the door. Taking a deep breath and readying myself to snap at the woman, I opened the door and stopped short when I found Cassian standing on the other side.

"Cassian? I thought you were headed back to Ravenshire?"

Cass shook his head as I let him in. Raph came over to me once the door was closed, placing his arm around my waist as I turned to face Cass. "What's wrong?"

Cassian's hair was in a disarray and April was nowhere in sight. Shit. Had something happened to her? "Is April okay?"

"Hmm? Oh yeah, she's just...looking around," Cassian said sounding extremely distracted. He was starting to freak me out.

"I can't go back, Jai," he murmured softly, a desperate look on his face that I'd never seen before.

"Do you not want to go back? Because I get that. You can stay here as long as you want," Raph offered and I squeezed his arm in thanks.

"No, it's not...I don't know what it is but...something is pulling me back. Every time I tried to leave, it was like something was tethering me to this town. I can still feel the tug. I don't know where it wants to lead me but I know what I have to do."

"What?" Raph asked just as I did and I squeezed his arm again, though I really wanted to give Cassian a hug right about now.

"I need to find out where this pull is coming from. I need to figure out what this pull *is*."

I looked up at Raph with a quirked brow, a question in my eyes. There weren't all that many pulls a mage felt in their lifetime, were there? The small smile and nod from Raph told me exactly what I'd suspected.

My wish was about to come true. My best friend won't be alone for too long now.

***

Curious where Fate will lead Cassian? Read his story in Sleep of Eternity.

ALSO BY STELLA

PARANORMAL ROMANCE

Set in Mistvale

Mages of Ravenshire:
Set in the fictional town of Mistvale, Mages of Ravenshire is a series filled with magic, laughs and love. Low on angst and high on sweetness, Mages of Ravenshire will leave you with a smile on your face. Come meet Neya, Pads, April, and all the other fur-babies and their humans, vampires and mages.

Touch of Magic. (Goofy mage x nerdy human)

Sleep of Eternity. (Grumpy mage x sunshine vampire)

Angel of Death. (Sweet necromancer x snarky vampire)

Boxset. (With a special bonus scene.)

***

Misfits of Mistvale:
With side-characters from Mages of Ravenshire, this series
features shifters, half-mermen, werewolves, and many more
supernaturals. With the usual dose of fur-babies, found family,
and all the Mistvale feels, this series features standalones with
a different couple in each book.

Claws. (Graysexual bobcat x cat shifter)

Tails. (Merman-siren x dolphin shifter)

Bonds. (Human x femme wolf shifter x asexual werewolf)

***

Mistvale Spin-Off Novellas:
Featuring various side-characters from the town of Mistvale,
these novellas are full of sweet, fuzzy romance, and the
meddlesome cast of Mistvale.

My Elf Mate. (GFY, holiday, elf x wolf shifter.)

My Dragon Mate. (Bi-awakening, human x dragon.)

My Elf Daddy. (Daddy/little, elf x human.)

My Fae Mate. (Genderfluid MC, holiday, Fate x Alchemist.)

<u>Make A Wish</u>. (Djinn x Human, free read.)

***

Set in Otherworld

Fate's Gambit Trilogy:
Fate's Gambit is an MMM PNR trilogy featuring a sweet, subby cinnamon-bun devil, a gentle-giant who's a service sub/Daddy switch, and a slightly frustrated Master as they slowly figure our their dynamic and fall madly in love. They're joined by annoyingly awesome side-characters including a sweet hedgehog, a sassy talking snake, and a guardian in the form of a cat-man. This trilogy features the same triad and needs to be read in order.

<u>First Play</u>. (Free Prequel.)

<u>Devil's Gamble</u>.

<u>Pet's Ploy</u>.

<u>Master's Design</u>.

<u>Boxset.</u>

***

Lords of Otherworld:
Following the events of Fate's Gambit, Lords of Otherworld delves deeper into the workings of Otherworld, with new characters, new romance, and new adventures. With found family vibes, danger and romance, each book in this series follows a different couple, with an overarching storyline. It is recommended to read the books in order.

<u>Maximus.</u>

<u>Zane.</u>

<u>Nox.</u>

***

Standalones

<u>Elijah Summons A Demon</u> (A newsletter serial.)

***

CONTEMPORARY ROMANCE

Voice Out

<u>Weathering The Storm</u> (Roommates to lovers, hurt/comfort.)

<u>Watching The Sunrise</u> (Friends to lovers, genderfluid MC.)

ABOUT STELLA

Stella Rainbow lives in a small town in India with her family and her five-year-old cat, Harry, who is her number one supporter, cuddle buddy, and writing buddy all rolled into one.

Living with a chronic illness, Stella grew up with books as her best friends, and now she writes in the hopes of giving others like her a reprieve from the real world.

Stella's books are low on the angst, high on the sweetness, with a doze of found family, and some absolutely adorable fur—and sometimes scale—babies.

You can join her <u>mailing list</u> to receive updates about her books and free content. You can also read more about Stella, her books, and the universe she writes in on her website, <u>www.authorstellarainbow.com</u>.

You can also follow her on:

Facebook: <u>Stella Rainbow</u>

Instagram: @authorstellarainbow
Goodreads: Stella Rainbow
BookBub: Stella Rainbow
Amazon: Stella Rainbow